666

"Here is wisdom. Let him that hath understanding count the number of the beast: for it is the number of a man; and his number is Six hundred three score and six." (Rev. 13:16-18)

Thomas Ethier

LIGHT SWITCH
P R E S S

Published by:
Light Switch Press
PO Box 272847
Fort Collins, CO 80527
www.lightswitchpress.com

ISBN: 978-1-939828-13-2

Copyright © 2015

Printed in the United States of America

Acknowledgement

This has not been an easy book to write, and if it were not for the encouragement and support of my family and friends, I am sure it would have been one of those novels started, but never finished. In that spirit, I would like to give special mention of a few *very* special people.

To my brother Phil, who gave me the inspiration and determination to make this book a reality! Without his example and spirit of perseverance, I would never have attempted the undertaking of, writing this book. Thank you for everything, Phil.

To Capt. Clayton Pearson, whose critique and editorial travails, kept me on the straight and narrow.

To Bobby Gilmore, posthumously. He is loved and missed by many. I pray he has found the happiness he deserves.

And finally, to all those who have, in ways they may never know, seen me through the difficult times, and contributed in making this book a reality.

Thank you, and my God bless!

Although some of the events in this book are shadows of actual events past, it in no way attempts to predict what will unfold in the future. Only God knows the future. It is a book of fiction, and should be read with that in mind. Any similarities to persons, dead or alive, places, and events are strictly from the imagination of the writer. In no way is it a representation of real characters. Scenarios of events are strictly imaginary. I hope you enjoy the book, and look forward to the next installment!

Roberto Etea

Introduction

Rune Mikkel was orphaned at birth with no knowledge of his true parents. He was raised in a Catholic orphanage in Rome, Italy until the age of 2, when he was adopted by a wealthy German couple. They named the boy Rune Mikkel after his adoptive fathers' grandfather. Rune was a good boy. He attended parochial school in Rome, graduated top of his class, and later attended college at a Roman Catholic University in Germany where he studied Economics and World Finance, and demonstrated a proclivity for religion, social sciences and economics. As a young adult, Rune was a soft spoken, healthy young man with dark brown hair, deep brown eyes, dark complexion, stood 6 feet tall with a muscular physique, and had a charismatic personality making him admired by peers and teachers alike. Growing up, Rune lived with his adoptive parents as any normal Catholic family with one very special exception. From a young age, Rune appeared to possess special talents and abilities bordering on the miraculous! These special gifts did not go unnoticed by the Church, and soon was brought to the attention of the Holy See. By the age of 14, the Holy Father in Rome had a watchful eye on the life of the boy. However, as time passed, Rune began to question himself and the source of his abilities. With the help of a life-long friend, he set out to discover the source of his gifts, starting with his roots and the identity of his true parents. With a chance meeting of an old friend, centuries of deeply guarded secrets, religious mysteries, and diabolical plans were slowly exposed, ultimately providing Rune with the truth, once and for all, of his true identity and the source of his miraculous powers.

Who is this Rune Mikkel? Some believed him a modern day prophet, others, the Son of God, and still others, the Anti-Christ. The truth, once revealed, will not only change *his* life, but that of the entire world... *forever*!

Prologue
Giza Plateau, Giza Egypt
1977

It was the end of a long, hard day, as Dr. Osborne stepped out onto the balcony of his hotel suite to get a breath of fresh air and clear his head. It was late September, and the cooler nights of autumn had yet to find its way into this desert oasis. The balcony faced west, providing him with a spectacular view of the setting sun, transforming the sky into various shades of yellows, orange and blues. But neither the splendor of the modern day architecture that surrounded him, nor nature's breathtaking painting of the horizon, could distract from this sacred place, the sense of the majestic and mysticism that has long been associated with it. As Mark held the black, cast iron railing of the balcony with both hands, he leaned into the evening air as a rare and welcomed breeze washed over his body. Closing his eyes, he felt transported in time to an ancient past, and swore he could hear in the distant wind, the sounds of chariots and the voices of the Pharos long departed. Cairo truly was a magical place. As he slowly opened his eyes, the reason for his being in Egypt once again overpowered his thoughts, and the tranquility he found in his escape of the present was replaced with emotions of guilt and disdain. He compromised his morals, his ethics, and betrayed all he held sacred to his chosen profession. Being an archaeologist was all that he ever wanted to be. But he was too impatient! He was too easily seduced into taking the quick path to recognition and fame, and that was something he now realized he would regret for the rest of his life. But it was too late to do anything about it. Much too late!

Tomorrow, he and Dr. Hilterman would breach the hidden chamber, ending an almost 2 year illegal dig – a dig conducted without the knowledge or authorization from the Egyptian government, in one of the most sacred and prohibited sites in all of Egypt.

It all began in the summer of 1975 when Mark, along with a Forensic Anthropologist, Dr. Fronz Hilterman (a one-time friend and colleague of Marks')

were approached by a private agent representing an undisclosed benefactor, with an offer to lead a dig of an unprecedented nature. Mark and Dr. Hilterman were offered the opportunity to be the chief Archeologist and Anthropologist on what was possibly the most unusual, if not secretive dig, Mark ever conducted, not to mention one of the most expensive. The most remarkable thing about the dig, as far as either man was concerned, was the secrecy surrounding it. Neither man was given much information, despite the fact they would be leading the expedition. They did not know the name of their benefactors. They did not know what they were searching for, other than a hidden chamber. They did not know what the chamber was supposed to contain. The area in which the dig would take place was highly protected and prohibited from archeological excavations of any kind, by order of Egypt's Supreme Council of Antiquities and the Egyptian Ministry of Culture, who had absolute authority in these matters. It was also apparent that someone within these very prestigious offices was paid a great deal of money to look the other way, allowing the dig to proceed without interference from either agency. If the dig *was* "discovered", it could destroy the reputations, and put an end to the careers of both Mark and Dr. Hilterman, and would most likely put both of them in an Egyptian prison for a very long time. Nonetheless, having the opportunity to conduct a dig in the Giza Plateau, culminating at the feet of the Great Sphinx itself, was something he would sell his soul for. It was an opportunity of a lifetime, and one that neither man had the power to resist.

Not knowing who his benefactors were, or what they hoped to find in the chamber, was always of great concern to Mark. Since the dig was not authorized by any legitimate office in Egypt, he was certain the motivation for the dig was not for the benefit of furthering the study and science of antiquity. Nor was it likely that financial gain be the motivation, considering the extreme cost involved in the project.

Mark, like all good archeologists, had an innate aptitude as an investigator, as well as possessing an unquenchable curiosity. So it was not surprising that he took it upon himself to seek out the identity(s) of the benefactor(s), and hopefully discover the true purpose of the dig. He hoped that once revealed, he could justify his actions and risks, and help ease his guilty conscience for betraying his ethics and dishonor to his profession.

Since it was obvious from the start that Mark would not be able to undertake this investigation alone, (most of his time would be spent on the dig itself), Mark sort out the assistance of a close friend and renowned investigative reporter named James Claiborne. James not only possessed both the talent and skills needed for the job, but also was not without connections in local and foreign governments that might prove invaluable at opening doors otherwise inaccessible to most people. Mark was confident he could trust James to keep the investigation and any information he may discover strictly confidential.

A file, the whereabouts known only by the two men, was created, which contained all the information either man could verify, no matter how disconnected or random it may have seemed, relating to the dig. This included names, places, events and time sequences.   What follows is a copy of that report.

Discovery of the Chambers Existence: How, When, Who?

The following information was provided to Mr. Claiborne by a close friend who served under Mr. Claiborne during the Korean War and is now working for the Secret Service. This information was provided at great risk for the operative, and all steps to keep his name anonymous will be taken.

- *In 1974, the United States was conducting secret satellite surveillance of the Middle East. A new sophisticated spy satellite capable of penetrating deep within the Earths' surface was used to search for hidden underground storage facilities capable of stockpiling weapons of mass destruction. The top secret Hexagon System Satellite, believed capable of only topographical surveillance, was in reality capable of, with the use of sophisticated subsonic equipment, identifying hidden underground chambers and bunkers,*

- *as well as the chemical signatures of most biological, chemical, and nuclear weapons.*

- *While doing surveillance over the Giza Plateau, a small chamber measuring 10 by 25 meters was discovered approximately 20 meters below the right foot of the Great Sphinx. No means of entry or exit*

*could be detected, and although it appeared obvious that the chamber
held contents undetermined, analysis for trace elements of weapons
of mass destruction proved negative. As a result, the fully operational
(SSSCC) Stealth Satellite Strategic Command Center (a top secret
military command center that would not be legitimately acknowledged
for years to come) dismissed the discovery and labeled the find as benign,
maintaining a copy of the file for future reference in the event of any
change.*

Possible Sale of Information

- *Although never proven, it was suspected by the Secret Service that
the files containing the information about the chamber was accessed
by the SSSCC's Deputy Commander Colonel Cornel Wiseman who sold
the data and all the files with related satellite printouts, to individual(s)
unidentified. Summarily, Colonel Wiseman took early retirement, and the
only existing files, including the satellite printout showing the location
of the hidden chamber, was in the hands of person or persons unknown.*

The Offer

*The following information comes from direct knowledge of the events by
the principle(s) involved.*

- *In stealth manner, Dr. Mark Osborne and Dr. Fronz Hilterman were
approached by a gentleman who ultimately orchestrated an agreement
for both Dr. Osborne and Dr. Hilterman to conduct a clandestine dig
in exchange for financial consideration to include an unlimited expense
account, and full future recognition for the find.*

- *All workers for the dig were to be supplied by the benefactor(s).*

Each man assigned to work the dig, although professionally unknown by either Dr. Osborne or Dr. Hilterman, appeared capable and experienced archeologist. All claimed to have less information about the details of the dig than either Osborne or Hilterman (something Mark had reason to doubt). Each worker followed orders blindly and without question.

- *Neither Osborne nor Hilterman ever heard from the man who contacted them again. All future correspondence was handled via special courier, and all money exchanged through a Swiss bank account.*

Conditions of the Agreement

- *Both Mark and Fronz were forbidden to make known or discuss any aspect connected to the dig to anyone, at any time, until released from the contract by the benefactors. To do so would mean immediate halt to the project and protection from prosecution by Egyptian authorities.*
- *Except for mandatory daily reports on the progress of the dig, Mark and Fronz were given complete autonomy in every aspect of the dig with one exception. Additional manpower, if needed, regardless of purpose, was to be provided by the benefactor(s) alone.*

End of Report

Nearly two years have passed, and tomorrow was the day they would finally reach the chamber, and the cloak of mystery that still remained would finally be lifted.

Upon returning to the hotel after a long day in the tunnel, Mark was handed an envelope that was left anonymously with the desk clerk. Leaving the balcony and returning to the small but comfortable living area of his hotel suite, Mark took the envelope, poured himself a drink of scotch and water, sat at the desk and opened it. Inside were several old newspaper clippings and a photo. Mark looked at the photo first. He immediately recognized the picture. It was the man who originally contacted him about the dig, now identified in a clipping attached to the photo as Charles Schmitt, (Mark never knew the man's name). The brief article told about his apparent suicide which took place, according to the article, only days after his meeting with Mark and Fronz. The word, "Illuminati", was written across the photo. That was a word Mark had not heard since his college days, when he did a paper on the history of the Roman Catholic Church. After studying the photo and re-reading the article several times, Mark picked up the other clippings. The first dealt with the investigation of the death of Colonel Cornel Wiseman, a name Mark recognized from his own files, who died under mysterious circumstances only weeks after he retired and moved to an Island off Central America.

Another article told about the disappearance of billions of dollars from the Banco Ambrosiano, a bank located in central Italy, in early 1974, ultimately leading to its collapse. Mark noted that this was the approximate date of his encounter with "Mr. Schmitt".

A third article focused on alleged ties between the Banco Ambrosiano and the Vatican Bank. The article described a criminal law suit accusing the Vatican Bank of providing letters of reference for non-existing companies in Latin America to the Banco Ambrosiano, in order to help secure loans for billions of dollars; money that later completely disappeared and was a major factor leading to the collapse of the Banco Ambrosiano.

The last article alleged connections between Hoberto Calvine, Director of the Banco Ambrosiano, and key financial officials in the Vatican. Stapled to the article was another, dated 4 weeks later, showing the body of Hoberto Calvine, hanging from under a bridge just outside of Rome. Again the word "Illuminati" was written across the photo.

Finally, the envelope contained a list of names, many, but not all of which, were priests or bishops, as well as a few politicians and international bankers. A few of the names were familiar to Mark, but only by reputation. There was no explanation as to the connection between the people on the list with any of the other articles or the photo found in the envelope.

Who would be sending this information to him, and what connection, if any, it had to the dig, Mark did not know.

Someone knew he and Fronz were involved in an illegal dig, and, at the moment, that was more of a concern to Mark than anything else. It also crossed Mark's mind that this may be a warning of some kind that he and Fronz were in danger – perhaps mortal danger! Mark knew he had no other option but to share this information with his partner, and the sooner, the better.

The hotel suite that Mark had been staying at for the past two years was the Le Meridien, about 15 miles from the entrance of the dig. It was a first class hotel, although the rooms were small. He chose this hotel strictly for its location. He needed someplace inconspicuous, considering the covert nature of his activities, and his choice worked out better than he had hoped. Besides having excellent air conditioning, (a major consideration during the summer months in the desert), his suite was nicely furnished with a large desk that served as a work station, and was reasonably quiet. Although the hotel staff was friendly and accessible, they were not intrusive, and that provided Mark with plenty of needed privacy. He could leave and return without attracting attention, since the hotel was a favorite of tourist interested in sightseeing tours of the Great Pyramids of Giza and the Sphinx.

Mark phoned his partner Fronz, and when unable to make contact, left a message for Fronz to meet him at the hotel as soon as possible. He was becoming uncharacteristically nervous as he continued to review and reflect on the contents of the envelope, and contemplating the meaning when a loud knock at the door caused him to spill half his drink. He wiped his hands on a towel from the bathroom, than crossed the small living space, which furnished, besides the desk, a loveseat, with decorative coffee and end tables. He opened the door.

"Mark, my friend." said Fronz as he entered Marks' suite. Fronz was a large man, standing just over 6 feet 3 inches tall. He was of German descent with a deep German accent, short cropped blond hair, blue eyes and a rugged physique. Like Mark, Fronz loved Egyptian culture and completed postgraduate work in Forensic Anthropology at the University of Liverpool. It was during his third year at the University, that he and Mark met on a dig in Egypt. A longtime friendship ensued.

"I received your message and came as soon as I could." He grasped Marks right hand in both of his and shook. "You sounded upset on the phone. Is everything all right? You have me worried."

"I'm sorry Fronz, it's probably nothing. Please sit down. I have something I'd like you to see." Mark said. Fronz took a seat as Mark walked over to the small, but well stocked bar, and refreshed his drink. "Can I get you something to drink?" he asked Fronz?

"A Black Russian, please." he said. Mark made the drink for Fronz and refreshed his own. He walked over to Fronz, handing him his drink and the envelope, along with a copy of the file he and Mr. Claiborne assembled on their investigation over the last two years. "You need to take a look at these." he said.

Fronz took the file and envelope, sat at the desk and started to read. He looked over everything very carefully and then turned his attention to the file of the investigation by Mark and Mr. Claiborne. When he finished, he laid both the file and the contents of the envelope on the table. He looked up at Mark with confusion. "I don't understand. Where did all this come from, and what is it supposed to mean?"

"I don't know where the envelope or its contents came from, they were left this morning with the desk clerk, anonymously." Mark said. "As far as the other files, they belong to me. It contains information I, and an associate whose name I don't wish to disclose, uncovered in an investigation I initiated when we first began the dig two years ago."

"You mean you have been investigating our benefactors and you never told me? Why? I mean I've always known that you have this incredible curiosity, but you know how important absolute secrecy of what we're doing is, especially to our benefactors. If they ever found out you were trying to discover their identity, it would blow this whole operation for both of us. Is it that important for you to know who is paying the bills?"

"Yes it is." replied Mark. "And not only who, but why? Why spend millions of dollars on a dig, unless you have some idea of what will be found? And why keep that a secret from us? What do they expect to find that is worth all that money, and incredible risk?

"And this envelope is proof that someone else knows we're here and what we're doing. More importantly, I believe that whoever that is, feels we are in some kind of danger. That is the only reason for sending it to me. It's a warning Fronz, it has to be. It's no coincidence that this was sent the day before reaching the chamber. And look at the date of this article." Mark handed Fronz the article reporting on the apparent suicide of Charles Schmitt. "This is dated only days after we last saw him. And did you notice the word "Illuminati" written across the photo?"

"What about it?" asked Fronz.

"The Illuminati is a secret society, supposedly hundreds of years old. It consists of men who were once leading members of the Church of Rome." explained Mark. "Surely you most have heard about them at some point in your studies and research."

"No, I don't believe I have." he said. "Besides, you know I have no time or interest in organized religion."

"They were wealthy, prominent men in the church; scientist, inventors, artists and philosophers. Men like Michael Angelo, da Vinci, Isaac Newton, to mention a few. These men were excommunicated, some executed, for their studies in science, which were in direct opposition with the teaching of the Church. They were forced underground in order to survive, and swore to get vengeance on the Church for what they had done. Legend has it, that they still exist today, and have played major roles throughout history in shaping and changing attitudes of the Church by infiltrating it and seizing control of the Holy See. They are even suspected in the assassination of several key Vatican officials, including more than one Pope. Their purpose was to place on the throne, those who would advance their goals of uniting science with religion and seek revenge for what they claimed was false persecution by the Church."

"What does any of this have to do with us, or with the dig?" asked Fronz.

"I don't know." said Mark. "But someone believes it does. Why else would I be given this information?"

"Mark, please." said Fronz. "You seriously believe that we are somehow involved in a conspiracy orchestrated by a secret society, bent on vengeance of the Catholic Church for excommunicating a few old men hundreds of years ago? Be reasonable Mark. The only reality here is that we have been given a great opportunity. It is true that our benefactors have chosen anonymity, most likely to avoid possible embarrassment, should the dig prove futile. Remember the American journalist who once had a promising future as an investigative reporter before he televised that 'Secret Vault' thing which turned out to be a dud? He never truly recovered from that fiasco. He should have kept his suspicions secret until he knew for sure what he had, or didn't have. I believe our benefactors are simply taking a lesson from history, and not counting their chickens before they hatch.

"We have a great opportunity to be credited for the find of the century and get our names on the list of academia. Don't come apart on me now! Forget this fantasy of conspiracies and secret societies. Live in the moment before you miss out on what may well be the best days of your life. Trust me my friend, finish your drink, take a hot bath and get a good night's sleep. Forget about this "Illuminati" business. You'll need all your wits about you tomorrow."

Mark glanced at the papers on the table. It was obvious that Fronz did not see the danger that he felt so strongly. Perhaps he *was* letting his imagination run wild. Although there was no doubting the photo and other contents of the envelope that lay on the table, maybe it was nothing more than some feeble attempt at blackmail from someone who discovered what they were doing. It may even be one of the laborers from the dig. He didn't know. Still, Mark had a sickening feeling deep in the pit of his stomach that it was much, much more. After years of investigation, the only two men Mark or James were ever able to connect the dig, Charles Schmitt and Cornel Wiseman, were branded as "Illuminati", and were now dead, and someone wanted to make sure he knew it!

Still, Mark thanked Fronz for coming over and apologized for bothering him and keeping him from his work. He promised Fronz that he would consider his advice and appreciated his candor.

Fronz rose from his chair and shook Mark's hand again and gave his friend a smile. "I'm sure I'm right about this." he said. "Clear your mind, get to bed early and have a good night's sleep. Tomorrow is going to be a big day for both of us. I can feel it in my bones!" said Fronz.

Mark walked him to the door and bid him a good night. He returned to the desk to finish his nightly report and his drink. When he finished, he sat back and thought about the day, his conversation with Fronz, and of course, the envelope. With nothing resolved, he decided to keep his promise to Fronz, and went to bed. Sleep would not come easily tonight, thought Mark as he turned off the bedside light.

Breaching the chamber

Mark sprang up in bed. For a moment he was not sure where he was. Then he heard the phone ring. He reached for the phone and realized that he was a little groggy and had a slight headache. Wondering what time it was, he looked at the clock by his bed. Ten thirty in the morning? It couldn't be! Mark was always up at the crack of dawn, and had never overslept in his entire life.

"Hello!" Mark said.

"Mark, is everything o.k.?" It was Fronz on the other end.

"Yeah, I guess I just overslept. Sorry, I'll be there as soon as I can. I should be about 30 minutes." Mark replied.

"No problem, we were just about to begin here anyway. I got a late start myself. I just got worried when you didn't show. It's not like you to sleep in, especially today." said Mark.

"I don't know what happened. Maybe I shouldn't have had that second drink last night. See you in a few." said Mark.

He hung up the phone and climbed out of bed with less vigor than what was his custom. He quickly showered, then dressed in long khaki pants, a light cotton shirt, and put on a pair of archeology site boots. He went to the refrigerator and poured himself a glass of milk, which he used to down 3 aspirins. Grabbing his Croatian camouflage backpack, and keys off the desk, he dashed out of the door and to his jeep. Never once had he glanced at the desk in his room, or notice that his personal files as well as the mystery envelope with all its contents were gone.

It was just before 11 AM when Mark arrived at the dig site, that, for security reasons, was located about five kilometers miles from the location of the hidden chamber shown in the satellite imaging provided to them. The tunnel was approximately three meters wide by two and one half meters high, and descended five meters down. Although the true destination lay southwest from the opening, the tunnel actually ran one hundred meters northeast, before navigating a complete one hundred eighty degree turn back toward the Great Sphinx. It took over twenty months to excavate the tunnel that now extended to within two meters of the hidden chamber, approximately four kilometers from the opening.

When Mark arrived, the workers were already busy removing the final wall of earth concealing the chamber. Excitement was practically tangible as anticipation of the breakthrough grew with each shovel of earth removed. Fronz emerged from the tunnel at the news of his partners' arrival, and quickly approached Mark who was climbing out of the jeep, carrying his backpack.

"Glad you could make it!" said Fronz with a smile. "The workers are in rare form this morning. It looks like we'll be breaking through in no time."

"I'm sorry Fronz." said Mark. "I don't know what happened. I've never overslept before."

"Forget it. You had a lot on your mind lately." said Fronz. "Besides, there is little you or I can do for the next hour or so anyway, except get some of this equipment set up." Fronz nodded to the left with a tilt of his head. There were several crates Mark had not seen before, piled close to the tunnel entrance.

"What's all this?" asked Mark as he walked over to the crates.

"They just arrived this morning," said Fronz, "along with these instructions". He handed Mark a large diplomatic pouch. He recognized it immediately as those used when they needed to communicate with the benefactors, or vice versa.

Mark opened the pouch and removed a folder which contained instructions for use of the equipment contained in the crates. Most of the equipment was high tech audio and video cameras, capable of two way communication, like those used by news cameramen on location. It would appear that the benefactors wanted to be witness to the breaking through of the wall into the chamber in real time. Mark could not help but wonder what they thought they would see.

Upon close inspection, Mark noticed that the crates were already opened. He started to go through the contents as Fronz approached him. "Have you ever used any of this type of equipment before?" he asked Fronz.

"Actually I have." he said. "I looked at most of it already. It's very similar to what I used on an expedition in Libya about four years ago. It's pretty simple to use, actually. If you like, I can run it myself. I'll only need help to get it set up. I'll have the workers move the equipment into position and we should be ready to go in about an hour or so."

"Sounds like you have it all under control." said Mark. "Let's get started." Fronz called three workers over and instructed them on what needed to be done. They quickly moved into action and within minutes the crates were swallowed up into the darkness of the tunnel as they made their way toward the chamber.

Mark sat at a makeshift table under the canvas top that was used mostly for shelter from the blazing sun while documenting the events of the day. He took a bottle of water from the cooler. It was ice cold and very refreshing. He opened the instructions sent in the diplomatic pouch once again and read them very carefully. It was detailed instructions on how to set-up the equipment that would provide a direct lead to a satellite dish to be found in one of the crates. By entering in an exact code, both the audio and the video feed would be picked up by satellite and broadcast live to the benefactors, origin still unknown. Mark made a quick scan of the area and noticed the satellite dish was already up and functional, just a little left of the tunnel opening. He was right. Fronz did indeed have it all under control.

Next, Mark reviewed the notes on the progress made the previous day, making additional notes about the events of the morning and acknowledged the receipt of the newly arrived equipment. He was getting excited about what the next few hours would bring, and his imagination was running wild. He tried not to think about this day for the last year or so, knowing it would be futile, and only drive him crazy. But now, with just hours left before reaching their goal, he could not stop thinking about what could be within the chamber, and the images of what might be, one after another, washed across his mind like waves at high tide.

"Mark." He heard Fronz call, breaking his train of thought and bringing him back to the present. "Are you ready? We should be heading down now."

Mark took a deep breath, put down his pen and looked at Fronz. "Let's do it." he said. He got up from his chair, walked over to Fronz and put a hand on his shoulder. "Let's see if we wasted the last 2 years of our lives, or if we are about to become the biggest news story since the discovery of the Rosette Stone."

"I'm with you," said Fronz as he slapped Mark on the back. Both men turned and headed down the tunnel. Perhaps Mark was still a little out of focus from being drugged the night before, or maybe he was too caught up in the excitement of the moment, but for whatever the reason, the silhouette of the gun, tucked away in Franz's jacket, went unnoticed.

In less than an hour, Mark and Fronz completed setting up the video equipment, as the workers were feverishly removed the last bits of earth concealing the chamber wall.

"I hit something!" yelled out one of the diggers. He was instantly joined by the remaining workers, four in total, followed by Mark and Fronz. After clearing a little more earth, they realized what they found was the outer wall of the chamber constructed from hewn stone.

Mark made a preliminary examination of the block and was surprised to see it was not the limestone most often used in the construction of the pyramids, or the Great Sphinx. Upon closer examination, he discovered a symbol

Mark recognized as the seal of the Knights Templar, and the following engraving, carved deep within the block:

Pauperes commilitones Christi Templique Solomonici
(Latin for "The Poor Fellow-Soldiers of Christ and of the Temple of Solomon")

Mark could hardly believe what he was seeing!

"Fronz, look here." Mark called. "Look at this inscription and the symbol. This stone has the seal of the Knights Templar! This can't be." he said. "There is no knowledge of the Templar ever constructing anything like this, at least not in this part of the world, during this time period. Look here. This stone was cut using the tools and craftsmanship associated with the Templars, and bares their marks, suggesting it was constructed and placed here some 800 years ago, 1,000 at most. Almost two thousand years after the Great Sphinx was built."

"No one touches anything." said Fronz with an authoritative command Mark had not heard before. "Mark, help me get this equipment operational. We have to get all this on film and connect with our benefactors before we remove another grain of sand."

Mark agreed and told the workers to clear as much of the area as possible in front of the stone, so they could have a clear field of vision and as much work area as possible.

As the workers cleared the area of all excess equipment and debris, Mark and Fronz quickly put the cameras and audio equipment into place. Fronz plugged the equipment into a portable generator and turned it on. Everything seemed to be working as expected. Next, Fronz connected the fiber optic line and antenna that ran the length of the tunnel to the outside satellite dish. Within minutes, they were in direct communication with someone that Mark assumed had to be one of the benefactors. It was obvious that this person knew Fronz by sight, and that Fronz had spoken with this man before. He was a man of stature, and had an air of importance, that was obvious. He appeared to be in his late fifties, maybe early sixties, with graying dark hair and dark eyes that gave a black appearance on the screen. He spoke with great authority.

"I'm here with Dr. Osborne, as well as all the workers." said Fronz. "As you can see, we have encountered what we believe to be the outside wall of the chamber. Dr. Osborne feels that the symbol engraved on the wall, among other things, indicate that the chamber may have been constructed by the Knights

Templar some 800 to 1,000 years ago." Fronz stood in front of the camera and pointed out the symbol on the stone for the camera.

"Of course I'll need time to do a more detailed inspection and perform some tests before I can be sure." said Mark.

"How much time Dr. Osborne?" said the unidentified man.

"I'm not sure." said Mark "A few days for sure, maybe a week if we can get started immediately. We want to make sure that we do this right."

"That won't be necessary." replied the unidentified man on camera. "Our interest lay outside the identity of the architect of the chamber, or its date at this time. We have sufficient video documentation for future examination if needed, and I am certain many more stones that comprise the chamber will afford you the opportunity for authenticity. At the moment, time is of the essence, and our interests are only in the contents of the chamber. You have my permission to breach the chamber now."

"I must protest!" said Mark. But before he could complete his objection, the unidentified man cut him off in midsentence. "Protest noted. The chamber will be entered now. If you wish, I will have Dr. Hilterman replace you as lead. It is your call Dr. Osborne, I will not waste any more time placating you."

Mark looked at Fronz in disbelief. It was obvious that his friend was not going to support him in any way on this. Fronz appeared dispassionate on the matter of preserving the site, and submissive to the wishes of their benefactor, regardless of the cost. Was it possible that Mark had misjudged Fronz so completely? How could he have been so wrong, so deceived?

Mark looked at Fronz, who remained acquiescent throughout the exchange never speaking a word or offering any support for Mark's position. "Very well." said Mark. "Take down the wall." he yelled to the workers as he stepped aside feeling defeated and betrayed.

It was like gold fever had taken over the workers as all proper archeological technique was abandoned and replaced by swinging crowbars and sludge hammers, chopping away as the stone wall, which stood as sentinel over the chamber for centuries crumbled. Mark could hardly speak, as he witnessed this sacrilege to archeology.

"We're through!" yelled one of the diggers, as he, with the help of the others, pulled down a corner of the stone. They quickly started to attack the opened area with hammers, pulling the crumbling bits of stone away, widening the opening even more.

A strange expulsion of air escaped the chamber as an eerie sound and the scent of age and decay was released, seemingly foreshadowing an unspoken doom that would follow. It stopped the workers for only a moment. Then they quickly returned to their reverent obsession of destruction. Within minutes, the crumbling remains of the wall was pushed aside, allowing access to the chamber for the first time in hundreds of years. Mark stood outside the chamber, staring motionless in disbelief and remorse at the destruction he witnessed, and watched as the dust slowly settled and the inside of the chamber slowly became visible.

Walking past Mark, Fronz stopped only a second at the entrance, then stepped through, being the first man inside the room in almost 1,000 years. Mark followed only moments later. He could not believe his eyes. He was correct about the chamber belonging to the Knights Templar, as a shield, crest, and swords, along with parchments and other identifiers were everywhere within the chamber. Centered in the room was a large stone vault with exquisite markings and inscriptions in Latin. Mark's eyes were glued to the writing, blocking all else from his mind. As he read the inscription, his face turned a grayish white and his eyes widened in disbelief. He attempted to call Fronz, but words failed him.

"I'm sorry Mark." said Fronz, as Mark heard what sounded like a magazine clip being slid into position. Mark slowly turned to see the weapon pointed directly at him. "Sorry it has to end this way my friend." Fronz said. "I really do like you, and you are one hell of an archeologist. You and I have a part in something much bigger than you can imagine. Something that began over 2,000 years ago, and you have fulfilled your role admirably. Now you have only one task left to perform. It will ensure complete secrecy until the appointed time. Your silence must be assured. My role is to see that you complete that task."

"What task?" asked Mark in a weak voice.

"to die, my friend." said Fronz. "Your last task is to die!"

Associated Press
Cairo, Egypt
8/24/1977

"A total of 6 bodies were discovered early Monday morning in a hidden chamber located 10 meters beneath the right foot of the Great Sphinx in the

Giza Plateau, Egypt," reported the AP. "Preliminary tests show 5 of the men were shot to death at close range, using what appears to be a German P08 Luger Parabellum, and one from a self-inflected shot to the head. Two of the men have been identified as Dr. Mark Osborne, a renowned archeologist, and Dr. Fronz Hilterman, forensic anthropologist of high repute, who appeared to have committed suicide after killing the other men at the site. Identities of the remaining victims are unknown at this time.

"It appears the chamber in which the bodies were discovered was accessed using a tunnel similar to those used by Mexican drug cartel to enter the United States.

The tunnel measures less than three meters square, four kilometers long and five meters in depth, originating northeast of the Great Sphinx. The chamber, which was unknown to exist prior to the gruesome discovery Monday morning, was empty. It is unclear as to what, if anything was removed from the chamber at this time."

"This was a very sophisticated operation, using the best equipment and experienced diggers." said the Head of the Supreme Council of Antiquities.

"The cost of such an operation must have been enormous. This could not have been perpetrated by a single entity. To have accomplished a dig of this magnitude undetected is unimaginable. I intend to conduct a full scale investigation and have enlisted the help of Interpol. I will get to the bottom of this outrage. Any artifacts stolen will be returned to the Egyptian people and the criminals punished, I promise you that." he said.

"So far, the only evidence discovered outside of the 6 bodies, was an ancient medallion found in the possession of Dr. Osborne, who authorities believe may have led this unlawful expedition. Although the medallion is not of Egyptian design, it is believed to be approximately 1,000 years old, and a valuable piece of evidence. Any further description of the medallion is being withheld at this time."

Chapter 1
Present Day

I suppose I should begin with how I first met Rune. It was in the first grade, so I was about five or six years old. I was going to Saint Francis International Elementary and Secondary School in Rome. Rune was transferred to our school about four weeks into the school year. He and his parents moved to Rome from Frankfurt, Germany. His father, Mr. Rolf Mikkel, was some kind of international banker and traveled frequently throughout Europe. His mother, Elsie Mikkel, was a stay at home mom, albeit with five house staff and a chauffeur at her disposal. They lived in the largest house I had ever seen. It must have had over thirty rooms which included servant quarters, indoor and outdoor pools, a tennis court and horse stables. I lived in the same neighborhood, but our home was nothing like his. We lived comfortably, but modestly. My dad was a journalist and recipient of the Pulitzer Prize for his paper on a Middle East Treaty with Jordan. My mother died when I was about three years old from breast cancer. Despite my young age at the time of her death, I remember her well and miss her a lot.

Mr. and Mrs. Mikkel was a handsome couple. Dr. Mikkel was six foot four inches tall with short cropped blonde hair and deep blue eyes. He had a rugged build and looked as if he spent many hours at the gym, but truth be known, his physique was due more to a good genetic pool than pumping iron.

Mrs. Mikkel also had blonde hair which she mostly wore up in French braids, and although she stood a respectable five feet eight inches, her height seemed dwarfed when standing next to her husband. She had blue eyes, although not as deep in color as her husbands, with a light complexion and a slim figure. Despite having servants to help around the house, she was a hands-on wife and mother, always keeping busy with the house and raising Rune. She kept active in the community as well, helping with fundraising and heading various committees.

Rune, on the other hand, looked nothing like his parents, reason being he was adopted. He never knew his true parents, who were killed in a car accident a week after he was born. Rune was small for his age as I remember. He had dark brown hair and brown eyes. His complexion was darker than either of his adoptive parents, and he had a frail appearance, but that was something he would soon outgrow.

Now you might think that Rune, being raised by such wealthy people and an only child, might be spoiled. But nothing could be further from the truth. Rune was a well-mannered, well behaved, and well liked boy. He made friends easily and even as a child, was generous to a fault. But the most remarkable thing I remember about Rune was how intelligent he was. His teachers were always amazed at how quickly he would grasp new ideas as well as his comprehension regardless of the subject matter. That was especially true with language and math, which he showed a particular proclivity. I later learned that his parents hired private tutors for him at home, each specializing in a particular subject matter. Although this was a contributing factor in his academic success, it was Rune's exceptional aptitude and interest for learning that made it work.

Still, despite all the hours he spent on studies, his play time did not suffer. His parents (more his mother, I think) felt just as committed to Rune's social development as they were to his academic success, and that meant an appropriate amount of play time and interaction with other children his own age. He especially liked soccer, as did I. I think that was the root of our friendship.

For Rune, Sundays were always kept open for church and related activities. The Mikkel's were devout Roman Catholics, and held strongly to the belief of keeping the Sabbath Day for worship only. Rune went to Mass from 8:00 to 9:00 am, followed immediately by Catechism until 10:00. Afterward, there would be a social gathering of fellow parishioners at his family's estate. A lunch would be served, after which, they would return to church for bible study that was usually followed with a lecture from a guest speaker. Then it was home for dinner, followed by one last visit to church for evening Mass. Once at home for the night, usually not until around 9:00pm, the family would spend some quiet time together and reflect on the lessons of the day. As in everything else, Rune showed an impressive understanding of religion for his age that even amazed his parents.

Rune and I became best friends, and though I was slightly older than he by a few months, taller and broader, it was Rune who became the Alpha person in our relationship. That suited me just fine. Not that I was the passive type. Far from it! It was just that Rune exhibited a natural leadership that somehow seemed right. Now that I am older and look back on it, I see it was very unnatural, having that type of control and influence at such a young age, I mean. But then again, hind sight is 20/20, isn't it?

Our childhood, as I am sure with yours, passed quickly, and before we knew it, we were in our 8th year of school. Rune and I had remained best friends and by then were practically inseparable. I was beginning to shoot up, measuring just shy of six feet. Not bad for a boy of thirteen. Unfortunately I was pretty slim, and with my red hair, I looked more like a huge animated carrot than a budding soccer athlete. Rune, on the other hand, outgrew the frailty of his boyish physique and now stood around five feet six inches tall and weighed around one hundred and twenty pounds and was developing a muscular physique that the young girls were beginning to notice. We were both on the school soccer team. I was the Captain.

It was during this time, in our eighth year at IESI, that Rune gained the attention of nearly everyone in our community, as well as the Catholic Church. It was the year Rune and I, along with about thirty other boys our age, were to receive the Sacrament of Confirmation at Saint Augustine Church in Rome.

Now as it happened, Mr. and Mrs. Mikkel were close friends with the Bishop of our Diocese, Bishop Paul Heiss. As a matter of fact, Bishop Heiss spent many Sundays with Rune and his parents as a guest at their estate. The Bishop, like everyone who knew Rune, was impressed with his comprehension of subject matter, especially as it related to the Holy Scriptures. He was unlike anyone the Bishop had ever met before, and it was for that reason he asked Rune to read the Epistle during the service following the administration of the Rites of Confirmation. This was a very rare privilege indeed.

Speaking in public, like everything else, came easy for Rune, so it was no surprise that he accepted the offer with all due humility, and looked forward to the honor. If it were me, I would have been scared shitless and would have tried my damned best to get out of it!

On the morning of the ceremony, the church was packed. The Mass was to be performed by Bishop Heiss himself, and when word of that got out, there was standing room only. Even parishioners only seen at Easter and Christmas services showed up. The church was beautifully decorated. It looked more like a cathedral to me, with tall steeples, life sized statues, stained windows and large vases filled with flowers that cascaded over the altar and lined the walls. There were huge medieval looking chandelier lights hanging from the rafters. They had frosted white glass, encased by black gothic design metal. One hung over every third row of pews, casting the church in a tenth or eleventh century atmosphere. The lit candles that covered the top of the altar, reminded me of the Jewish Menorahs, except each were gold in color and formed a "V" shape. A crimson carpet was laid down the aisle that ran from the front door, all the way to a breathtaking marble altar railing, delimiting the chancel of the church. As recipients of the Holy Sacrament of Confirmation, we occupied the first two rows of pews before the altar. We sat, and nervously anticipated the moment when we would be called to the altar and profess our faith, presenting the Church with our chosen name for confirmation.

The Mass proceeded as expected, each of us being confirmed with our new, personally chosen name. I chose Matthew, making my new Christian name Robert Joseph Matthew Claiborne. I don't know where I would ever use the name "Matthew" again. Rune chose the name Paul. His new Christian name was now Rune John Paul Mikkel. Sounds spiritual, doesn't it?

After receiving Communion (which took an exceptionally long time due to the large attendance), the choir sang a most inspiring hymn, after which Bishop Heiss approached the podium and announced that the closing Epistle would be read by the newly confirmed Rune John Paul Mikkel. I remember thinking that this would probably be the last time Rune would ever be called by his new name as well.

A hush overcame the congregation as Rune opened his Bible and began.

"A reading from the Epistle of Paul, Acts 2, verses 1 thru 16."

"When the day of Pentecost had come, they were all together in one place.

And suddenly from heaven there came a sound like the rush of a violent wind, and it filled the entire house where they were sitting. Divided tongues, as of fire, appeared among them, and a tongue rested on each of them. All of them were filled with the Holy Spirit and began to speak in other languages, as the Spirit gave them ability......"

Almost immediately after Rune began his reading, the congregation was buzzing with whispers which, with every verse he read, grew louder. People were shifting in their seats, some excited, some frightened.

I looked at Rune from my seat in the front pew, along with the other boys in our class, in complete astonishment, as Rune, oblivious as to what was happening, continued reading as if nothing out of the ordinary was occurring. Within minutes, half the congregation was on their feet, some were leaving, and a few of the Women (mostly the older generation) were crying. When Rune finally concluded his reading of the Epistle, he looked around the congregation and noticed, for the first time, what was happening. He was confused, and for the first time since I've known him, appeared to be at a loss for words.

Bishop Heiss quickly rose to his feet and approached the podium, blessing himself along the way. When he reached Rune, he put both hands on his shoulders and reassured him everything was all right, and told him to take his seat. Rune returned to his seat, which was next to mine, as Bishop Heiss addressed the church.

"Please, sit down." he said. "Let us remember we are in the house of the Lord. Please take your seats and be silent." It took a few minutes for things to quiet down, during which time, I turned to speak to Rune.

"What the hell was that?" I asked.

"What are you talking about? What is wrong with everyone?" he asked.

"Don't you know?" The look on Rune's face told me he had no idea what just occurred.

Our congregation was made up of members from many different cultures and backgrounds. Some were Italian, some French, German, English, Russian and Spanish. A few of the members were converted Jews who spoke Hebrew and Aramaic. And Rune had just read the entire Epistle, speaking in tongues! Oh, not like those you hear in most other services, where men and women raise their hands and shout out words and sounds that nobody understands, speaking the language of angels, they claim. No, Rune spoke in tongues as the Apostles did on the first day of Pentecost. He spoke in fluent Italian, as heard by the Italian members of the congregation, but he also spoke in French, heard by the French, as well as German, English, Russian, and Spanish, each member from those languages hearing him speak as if born to the language. He even spoke Hebrew and Aramaic, all at the same time. Yes, each man, women and child heard him speak in their own language, even their own dialect, and speaking flawlessly. Everyone from the eldest to the youngest heard him. And all the time, unknown to Rune who thought he was speaking in English.

"We are all truly blessed," said Bishop Heiss, "for the Lord Himself has chosen us worthy to be witness to the power and absolute authority of His Holy Spirit over us all. For today, the Lord has bestowed upon his servant, Rune John Paul Mikkel, the gift of tongues as given on the Day of Pentecost to the Apostles, testifying to the faith, conviction and acceptance of his servant to the Almighty God, His Son and His Holy Spirit. Each of you must look upon this as a personal sign. Let it be a light in your heart as a flame of faith and let no man put it out. Let each of you, man, woman and child who are witness, spread to all who will listen what the Holy Spirit has done here today. Not to the glory of Rune John Paul Mikkel, for he is but a tool, a vessel for use by God, but for the glory of the Lord forever and ever, Amen."

The entire congregation let out a loud "Amen" as everyone knelt in prayer, as the choir sang out with the voices of the Angels.

Now if this happened to me, I would have freaked out! But not Rune. No, he knew something extraordinary happened to him, and that he had been chosen, in a personal way unheard of for centuries. Yet he was determined not to let this define who he was. As far as he was concerned, nothing had changed for him. God simply used him to make a point, and he hoped that somehow, someway, it made a difference in someone's life. Maybe it could help to turn someone around, or restore a lost faith. But that was the end of it as far as he was concerned. This was the true humility of Rune as I knew him.

The Bishop, on the other hand, had an entirely different outlook on the whole situation. Once home, Rune was joined by his parents and Bishop Heiss to discuss what had happened that day and the meaning behind it.

"This is a sign from God." the Bishop said. "It should not be taken lightly. You have been chosen for some special purpose so far known only by God."

"Why me Bishop?" asked Rune. "Surely there are many men, you for one, far more worthy. I am just a boy with no greater faith than any of you."

"You know the scriptures as well as anyone I ever met Rune, so you know God does not choose a man by his works, for 'God is no respecter of men'. And as for the rest of us, God has a purpose for us all. Even if we are not sure at the moment what that might be. The fact is, Rune, you have been chosen. You may not understand it, you may not even like it, but that is of no consequence. God has a special purpose for you, and you can no more escape your fate than Jonah could outrun his."

"What should we do Bishop?" asked Mr. Mikkel. "We trust your judgment on this matter."

"First I must return to Vatican City and speak of today's event to the Holy Father." said Bishop Heiss. "He has probably heard rumors of it already, and will have many questions. Rune will be entering high school after summer break, is that not true?"

"Yes, that is true Bishop." answered his mother. "He will be attending Saint Francis here in Tivoli."

"I do not wish to speak for the Holy Father, but it may be that He would prefer if Rune attended a school other than Saint Francis. Saint Francis is an excellent school. I am not sure, however, if it can provide the guidance Rune needs. It might even be His Holiness's wish to allow Rune entrance into the monastery despite his youth to afford him special guidance. But I speak presumptuously. I am sure our Holy Eminency will wish only that which is best for Rune, and of course, what is the will of God."

At least that is how I remember it, as it was told to me by Rune. He really didn't want to leave Saint Francis and all his friends, but Rome was not that large, and could be crossed on a day trip. His father said that he would get a place closer to his school so Rune could still be with them whenever possible. It seemed it had all been decided, and Rune really had very little choice, if any. He would have to leave Saint Francis and his friends, in order to discover the meaning of this "miracle" bestowed upon him.

I didn't see Rune for almost a week after that day in church. There was a write- up in the local newspaper and even a short mention on the local news stations, but Rune and his family tried to play down the whole "miracle" thing as much as possible. It seemed to me that was in direct opposition to what Bishop Heiss told us to do at the service, when he said we should tell everyone about what we saw and be a personal witness to the event and all, but I wasn't going to say anything. Rune was still getting plenty of attention and recognition at church, as well as the community in general, but after a while, things started to quiet down, and resumed a more normal existence. Still, I felt kind of bad for him, because of all the people I knew, Rune was the most lest likely to want the spotlight. It was difficult for him avoiding the questions and explanations from everyone he encountered. I personally tried to keep my questions to a minimum, not wanting to add to his discomfort, but I must admit, I never looked at Rune quite the same way again. I always knew there was something special about him, and I had a feeling that it would not be the last time I would hear about the "miraculous" when it came to Rune John Paul Mikkel.

That summer passed quickly and soon Rune and his parents were packing in preparation for their move. Rune's father found a nice house, not as big as the one they now had, but it was close to the monastery Rune would be staying at, and Vatican City was only ten miles away. This proved convenient, since

Rune, who had already been presented to the Holy Father, was destined to be a frequent visitor. Rune was a little uncomfortable at first living at the monastery, but he was spared the solitude and confines of the monks and was allowed more freedom, at least to some degree. However, his religious studies, along with his secular education was taxing, even for him.

As it turned out, the "gift of tongues" was not a one-time deal. That is to say, since the day of his confirmation, Rune discovered he was able to speak fluently in over twenty languages, even though he never studied but three of them. For some time, that kept the spotlight on him, and that was not a comforting position for him to be in. Still, he liked his teachers, and was grateful for their guidance, even though at times it seemed they learned more from Rune than he did from them. Many of his private lessons were spent with Rune interpreting scriptures and answering questions. And there was something that bothered him. Rune was very apt at reading people, and although he couldn't put his finger on it, exactly, it appeared to him that his instructors, those that were assigned by the Vatican, had some kind of hidden agenda - some kind of secret that they were keeping from him. At the same time, if there was some special purpose that God had intended for him, he couldn't see it, at least not yet.

Chapter 2

For the next two years I got to see less and less of Rune, with him in Rome and I was still living in Tivoli, although we remained in contact through letters and e-mails. It was difficult to get him on the phone, (they discouraged phone calls at the monastery) and his heavy class schedules and tutoring kept him pretty busy. His dad, Mr. Mikkel, was also spending a lot of time with him, expanding Runes' social circle with people associated with Mr. Mikkel's business. I know that everyone wanted the best for Rune, but to me, they were making him grow up too fast. He had to quit playing soccer, and his new friends were usually older people or monks from the monastery.

As for me, I was doing all right. I was sixteen now, and focusing on what I wanted to do with the rest of my life. I wanted to pursue a career as a professional soccer player, but I just wasn't that good. And believe me when I say I tried! So instead, I decided on a career in journalism, following in my father's footsteps. I was very proud of my father and his work. As I already mentioned, he was recognized worldwide as a top investigative reporter and the recipient of a Pulitzer Prize in 1990. I fancied someday getting a Pulitzer for outstanding investigative reporting myself. I had big dreams!

The high school days were gone in a flash, and before I knew it, it was graduation day. **I graduated Cum Laude,** an accomplishment I was very proud of. I decided I would apply to the International School for Journalism at the City University of London, my father's Alma mater.

As I expected he would, Rune left the monastery, although discouraged to do so by the church. He decided to follow in his adoptive father's footsteps and attend Katholische Universitat Eichstatt-Ingolstadt, a Roman Catholic University in Euchstatt, Bavaria, Germany to study world finance. This made his adoptive father very proud, and that pleased Rune. Rune always felt he owed his parents a debt that could never be repaid, so to give them this pleasure was very rewarding to him. Rune liked the world of finance, and with the connections he made over the past four years through his father, he was pretty well situated for a promising future.

He was still very much involved with the church, as religion was a major part of his life. In his spare time he did volunteer work at a Catholic hospital where he provided spiritual counseling and would even help with direct care if they were short on staffing.

Now it was around this time I was beginning to take a deeper interest in girls. There was one girl in particular. Her name was Angela. We first met in my last year of high school, but were later reunited in London. She, like I, wanted to study journalism, although unlike me, she was the type that should be in front of the cameras, where I definitely belonged behind them. She had the face of angel, at least to me. She had silky blonde hair that fell about 4 inches below her shoulders and always seemed to smell of lavender. Her dark blue eyes and long lashes complimented her slim, petite face that always had just the right touch of rouge on her checks. She had a beautiful, sexy figure which I found most attractive. But the most amazing thing about Angela was the way she stirred feelings deep in my soul that I never felt before. And it was not just sexual either (although that was there as well). She always seemed to bring out the best in me; parts of me I never even knew existed before I met her!

The opposite sex did not elude Rune either. He would occasionally mention in his letters a girl that caught his attention. Maria Vallaitte was her name, and with the exception of my Angela, she was the most beautiful girl I had ever seen. She had long straight auburn hair that hung half way down her back. Her eyes were a deep blue with a light, smooth and luminous complexion. Angela and I met her on Spring break in our first year at college. We were invited to Rune's parents home for the week, and we hit it off from the beginning. Maria was a wonderful girl with a mind to match. I could see what Rune saw in her right away. They made a perfect couple. But Rune never indicated that their relationship was anything other than plutonic.

Now that I think about it, it was during that spring visit to Rune's parent's home when he first brought to my attention his concern about his private tutors. Even though he was no longer at the monastery, the Church continued to tutor Rune with a few hand chosen instructors in order to continue with his religious training in the doctrines of the Church. As I recall, Rune had mentioned to me that it appeared some of his tutors were infusing more science into their teaching than he would have expected. Not that Rune objected to the study of science, he actually enjoyed the lessons very much. It was just that, at that time, it seemed to him there was less emphasis on God, and more on science. This was especially odd since the beliefs and teachings of the Church were in decisive opposition to some of science, such as evolution vs. creation, the existence and immortality of a soul, abortion and stem cell research, just to mention a few. It also appeared to Rune that a few of his instructors were giving more credence to science than to Church doctrine. At times, he wondered if they might be testing him as to his willingness to accept science over the doctrines of the Church. But Rune's religious faith had always been the corner stone in his life and he firmly believed that if there was conflict between God and science, it was only because science hadn't advanced, or wasn't open minded enough, to comprehend and accept the truth. He always believed that someday, science would prove to its own satisfaction the existence of God, and that He is the sole source of all creation and the laws that govern it.

The second year at the University was exceptionally busy for me. I had no idea how much hard work went into being a good reporter. It seemed so easy for my father, who enjoyed his work so much. I was beginning to have more respect for his accomplishments with each passing day.

Besides classes, home studies and late nights spent on research, I was also required to travel, sometimes long distances, to follow and report on current events. I continued to see Angela whenever I could, and we spent school breaks and holidays together, with an occasional weekend thrown in. Our relationship had evolved to the next level and I was beginning to get very serious about her. I hoped the feeling was mutual. As it turned out, Angela and I had something besides our chosen careers in common. Something neither of us knew at the time. Both my and Angela's father worked together on a few occasions early in their careers, my father as a reporter and Mr. Shelton (Angela's father) as a photographer. This seemingly unimportant collaboration would ultimately play a major role in both our lives. But I digress.

I knew from his letters (it had been about six months since I had last seen him), that Rune was doing exceptionally well at the university and was gaining the attention of some very impressive financial gurus. Other than that, I was having less and less contact with him, mostly because we were both busy with our studies and personal lives. It felt like I was beginning to lose touch with Rune, and that was something I did not want to happen. We shared many things in our lives and I didn't want our friendship to become just a memory.

Then, around one week before Christmas in 2007, my third year at City University, I was assigned to cover a breaking news story in Rune's home town of Lazio, just outside of Rome, as part of my midterm final. This took me by surprise, and to tell the truth, I was a bit disappointed. There were many newsworthy stories from all around the world at the time that I was hoping to get assigned. The war in Iraq continued to garner worldwide attention, Hurricane Katrina, and its aftermath, spiraling oil and gas prices, just to name a few. But instead, I was to go to Lazio and interview witnesses to a residential fire that involved the rescue of a young woman under what some were calling a miraculous event. I was handed a preliminary report that read as follows:

"A woman on the 4th floor of a residential building, trapped by a blazing fire that engulfed the first three floors, was rescued by a bystander - a young man who rushed into the flaming building and returned a few minutes later leading the woman to safety.

'It was a miracle' claimed a witnessed to the rescue. 'It was like the story from the bible when the angel walked into the furnace and saved the three young men from a burning death. No one could have entered that building and survived. But *he* did !' "

"The woman was brought to fire fighters who immediately transferred her to a local hospital for evaluation. The rescuer refused any medical attention. Reports from the hospital stated that the woman (name being withheld by request) suffered no injuries. The young man disappeared into the crowd of bystanders as quickly as he appeared, but not before being identified by several witnesses as a local resident and student by the name of...'Rune Mikkel'. Attempts to contact Mr. Mikkel by local reporters have been unsuccessful."

I felt a chill over my entire body. My heart was pounding in my chest. Rune. I should have guessed. And who was the woman? Could it possibly have been Maria? I grabbed my equipment and called Angela on my way out the door. She would want to know about this, and with any luck, I could persuade her to accompany me to Rome.

I was fortunate enough to get a flight to Rome that afternoon. It was about a two hour flight from London to Rome, but it seemed much longer to me. I spoke with Angela on my cell, and although she agreed to meet me in Rome, she would have to catch a later flight. I welcomed the opportunity to see Rune again, but was uneasy about bringing up the reason for the visit. I didn't want to use our friendship as a way to get an interview he was obviously trying very hard to avoid. I also needed to keep this completely professional. How was I going to accomplish that? I would leave time to solve that mystery.

I spent most of the trip using my laptop, researching everything I could about the story. It was still fresh news, so I had some luck. The event was covered by several local news stations, and was on this new social media thing called "Face Book". I was able to find 6 printed articles in local newspapers. I knew Rune was trying to keep a low profile, but I was pretty sure the story would make the AP by night fall. It was a story that had sensationalism, mixed with personal drama that would appeal to the masses. I was also certain that the Vatican would hear about it as well, and that might make talking to Rune more difficult, without playing the friendship card.

I tried to reach Rune by phone and e-mail before I left for Rome, but only got through to his voice mail. I left a message and told him I was on my way to Rome and that I wanted to meet with him as soon as possible and asked if he would return my call. I left him my cell number; although I was sure he already had it.

A "*new message*" alert popped up on my screen. Not from my school or business e-mail account, but from my personal yahoo account. It was from Rune!

"Received your message. Look forward to seeing you. Send ETA and flight number. Will meet you at airport. Be great to see you again. Rune."

Well, that solved one problem. It looked like things just a got a lot easier for me. I e-mailed him back and gave him my ETA and also told him that Angela would be joining me in Rome as well, but on a later flight. I mentioned it would be great if Maria was around, so we could all get together for a visit. I only half expected a reply, and when none came, I decided to leave well enough alone. I would be seeing Rune in about one hour, and we could sort things out then. The rest of the flight to Rome was bumpy and full of turbulence. I wondered if it was a sign of things to come.

Chapter 3

I arrived in Rome at 4:55PM, about ten minutes ahead of schedule, and found Rune waiting for me at the terminal. He looked well, and genuinely glad to see me. We exchanged the usual greetings and handshake. Rune asked if I had any luggage, and I explained that I only had my carry-on, which was slung over my shoulder, and a briefcase, which contained my laptop.

"I realize that this is near the end of the school semester, but I was hoping that you would be able to stay for a while anyway." Rune said.

"I wish I could, but I'm afraid this will have to be a short visit. I am actually here working on an assignment for my final in Professor Heckerman's' class. I have two, maybe three days, and then I need to get back."

"Professor Hickerman, well I'm impressed." said Rune. "I know of his reputation as a top-notch journalist and instructor. I'm sorry to hear that this will be such a brief visit. What about Angela? You said that she will be joining you. Is she working this assignment with you?" Rune asked as we headed out of the terminal.

"I wish! That would guarantee me a passing grade. I asked her to come along because I was hoping to mix a little business with pleasure. All work and no play, you know. Is Maria going to be joining us?" I asked. "Angela is looking forward to spending time with her."

"She'll be stopping by my house in a little while." Rune said. "Robert, I have to ask. Does your assignment have anything to do with me?"

"You always could see right through me." I said.

"It doesn't take a genius to figure it out." he said. "Reporters have been calling, showing up at my home and even at the school. Fortunately their legal department was able to put a stop to it. The school claimed they were interfering with student studies, and their behavior was borderline harassment. The next thing I know, I get this phone message from you, who I haven't heard from in almost five months, and learn you're catching the next flight to Rome to see me. Let's see, how did you put it? 'I need to see you as soon as possible'."

"You make me feel guilty, and I'm not sure why." I said. "It's true, I am here because of the story about the fire a couple of days ago on Cathedral Square. And I did read you were there."

"And that I walked through fire, am I right?"

"Something like that." I said. "And the woman you saved. Was it by any chance Maria?"

"You're going to make a great investigative reporter Robert." he answered.

"Is that a yes?"

"That's a yes. But there is much more to the story than that. But this is not the time or place to discuss it. When do you expect Angela to arrive?"

"She's due to arrive at 6:15 on flight 203 from London." I said.

"Look, I'm parked outside. Let me take you to my place. I'll give Maria a call while you unpack. Then we can all take a ride out to meet Angela when she arrives."

"I was planning to stay at a hotel downtown. I don't want to put you out." I told him.

"Why? I have plenty of room at my house for you and Angela, and it will give us a better chance to talk. We don't get to see enough of each other. Let's take advantage of the opportunity that providence has provided."

"Aren't you living with your parents?" I asked.

"Not for the last several months now. Between school, work at the hospital and my private tutoring, I felt it best to have a place of my own so I wouldn't interfere with Mom and Dad's life. Always in and out, you know? Anyway, I found this great place downtown and there is plenty of room for both of you."

"What can I say? I accept. Thank you. Do you live far?" I asked.

"No, it's just a short drive." He said. "I live central to school, church and the airport, for convenience sake. Here's my car."

His car was a new silver Mercedes-Benz E. Not the type of car that I would have expected from Rune; not that he couldn't afford it. It just seemed a little pretentious for his personality. At least the Rune I grew up with.

"Wow, some car. Don't tell me you got this to impress the girls." I joked.

"I know it may seem extravagant," he said, "but to tell you the truth, it is one of the best built and most reliable cars on the market today. If you can afford it, it is the best buy for your money, and I would know, I am a financial wizard, or haven't you heard?"

"I've heard." I said. We both laughed.

We got inside the car and headed out of the city toward Lazio. Other than small talk, which was mostly about our families and school, the ride was a quiet one. I could tell that Rune was giving a lot of thought about how much he wanted to disclose to me about the events concerning the fire and rescue of Maria. I decided not to press him on the issue and instead be patient.

In less than twenty minutes, we were pulling into the driveway that I assumed lead to Runes' home. As it turned out, Rune was living in a modest, but comfortable house just outside the city. He wanted a comfortable place in order to focus clearly on his studies. His father wanted him to enjoy the lifestyle he was accustomed to while living with his parents, while allowing him the freedom and independence he needed to be his own man. It had three bedrooms, each with its own bath, a large living room, a den and well equipped kitchen. The shaded patio led out to a sizable back yard which was well manicured and had several meticulously pruned shrubs and hedges which provided complete privacy.

"I could get used to a place like this." I said.

"I know." said Rune. "It's a bit much, but you know dad. I told him I could make do with much less, but he wouldn't hear of it. He even wanted to provide a cook and maid service, but I put my foot down on that. You know I never liked the idea of having servants. I am capable of taking care of myself."

"I know." I said. "But this is a great place! I'm glad I decided to take you up on your offer. I will be much more comfortable here."

"Great!" he said. "Let me show you to your room."

He led me through the den and down a hall, where there were three doors. The first I assumed was Runes' bedroom. He opened the door to the second room, which was a large room, complete with a queen size bed, desk and chair, computer, phone, settee, large screen TV and a private bath. I put my bag on the bed and looked around. "Very nice." I said.

"If there is anything else you need, please let me know." said Rune.

"The only thing missing is a secretary and masseuse." I said in jest.

"Just a phone call away." he said with a big smile. "Why don't you freshen up, and I'll give Maria a call. If you're thirsty or want something to eat, help yourself to anything in the kitchen. But don't fill up. I am planning to take us all out to dinner once Angela arrives."

"That sounds great." I said.

Rune left and closed the door behind him. I unpacked the few things I brought and hung them up in the closet. I thought how nice it would be to be able to spend more time with Rune, but I knew I had to be back to London by Monday morning and submit my assignment. I must admit I felt a little ashamed of taking advantage of Rune and his generosity. After all, if truth be known, I wouldn't even be there if it wasn't for this damned assignment. I should have been there because I wanted to see Rune and Maria again, and not to make a grade. I promised myself I'd make it up to him somehow.

After freshening up, I headed to the kitchen and made myself a cup of coffee (the one true addiction I have except for Angela), and took the cup with me as I strolled out into the back yard. It was a truly beautiful place, and I meant it when I said I could get used to it here. I had just sat down when I heard the doorbell. I wondered if it was another reporter looking for Rune. It was Maria.

Rune opened the door. Maria was always beautiful, but in the year or so since I had seen her last, she had grown into a radiantly breathtaking, stunningly beautiful young woman!

Rune leaned forward and put both hands on Maria's shoulders and gave her a gentle kiss on her left cheek. The look in her eyes could only be described as someone in love. I felt guilty witnessing what appeared to be a tender and personal moment. I softly cleared my throat announcing my presence, and both Rune and Maria turned, looking my way.

"Maria, it's so good to see you again. And look at you. You look fantastic."

"It's so nice to see you Robert." she said.

I walked over to meet her and we embraced. "It has been too long."

"I agree." she said. "Is Angela here yet?"

"She gets in around 6:15." I said. "She is looking forward to seeing you. She misses you both as much as I do."

"We can pick her up at the airport, bring her back here to freshen up, than go out to dinner, if that's O.K. with you Maria?" Rune asked. "Then we can come back here and have a talk, if everyone feels up to it."

"If Robert and Angela aren't too tired." said Maria.

"It's only a two hour flight." I said. "I don't want to speak for Angela, but if I know her, she would like that as much as I would."

"Then its settled." said Rune. "Maria, would you like to keep Robert entertained while I take care of a few things? We can head out in about 15 minutes, so we can be there before Angela's flight arrives."

"I would like that. It will give us a chance to catch up on things." Maria said.

"Why don't we go onto the patio while we wait for Rune to make his phone calls. It's beautiful this time of year." she said.

"I know." I said. "I was enjoying the view before you arrived. Would you like something to drink before we go out?"

"No thank you. I'm fine. Just the fresh air is all I want. Shall we?" she asked, pointing to the patio door. I placed her hand over my arm and we made our way out to the patio.

"How did you know?" I asked.

"I'm sorry, how did I know what?" Maria asked

"That Rune had to make some phone calls?" I asked.

"Rune was right." she answered. "You are going to be a great reporter one day, like you father."

"I'm sorry." I said. "I didn't mean to pry. I guess I just don't know when to turn it off."

"That's all right." she said. "You're forgiven. But I think I will let Rune answer your questions if you don't mind. O.K.?"

"O.K." I said and quickly dropped the subject.

In a few minutes Rune returned and we set out for the airport. Angela's flight arrived on time, and we met her at the gate. It was great to see her. Somehow it made me feel more comfortable with her here. Not that I was uncomfortable with Rune and Maria. It was just different when Angela was around. I guess I was falling in love with her.

Anyway, Rune and Maria greeted Angela and welcomed her to Rome. We explained our plans for the evening and asked if she felt up to it, and as I suspected, she was. We drove back to Rune's, and he took Angela's suitcase to the bedroom at the end of the hall. It was furnished much like my room, with just a slight difference in color scheme. We gave her time to freshen up and unpack, and then we were on our way.

The restaurant Rune chose must have been one he frequented, because he was recognized immediately by the hostess. We were brought to a table with a fantastic view of the city. We ordered, and had a cocktail before dinner. The food was the best I have had in a very long time, and I could tell Angela felt the same way. We talked a lot about home, school, new friends and our families. It was good to just be together again, and we promised to do it more often. I never mentioned the story, not wanting to ruin the evening.

After dinner, Rune took us on a short drive, pointing out the highlights of the city and points of interest he thought we might enjoy on our visit. Then it was home for the night.

It was almost 11 PM when we got back to Runes, and I expected that any talk would have to wait for the morning, but to my surprise, Rune suggested coffee on the patio.

"If you are not too tired." he said.

"I'm fine, how about you Angela?" I asked.

"I'd love to." she said.

Rune excused himself as he went to get coffee, and the three of us went out to the patio. It was a beautiful night, despite the lateness of the season and hour. It only took a few minutes for Rune to return with coffee and some holiday cookies.

"Is anyone cold?" he asked.

We all agreed that the weather was beautiful and we were comfortable sitting outside.

"Great." he said. Rune took a seat next to Maria.

"I know that you want to ask me about the night of the fire. I spoke with Maria before you arrived, because I wanted to get her approval before I spoke, as this involves her as well." he said. "We both agreed we would like to tell you everything that happened that night."

"Before you begin," I said, "I would like to get this on tape if you don't mind. It helps me to not misquote anyone. But I want you to know that I will not print or discuss anything without your approval. I respect your privacy above all else, and will not use our friendship to take advantage of the situation. No one will ever hear this tape other than Angela and me."

"I appreciate that Robert." he said.

"As do I." said Maria. "We trust you both completely, that's why we agreed to talk to you. Besides, I am not sure that anyone would believe the truth anyway. I mean, it's hard to believe, even for me."

"This won't be the first time 'hard to believe' would describe something associated with Rune." I said with a smile.

"You mean the confirmation service and speaking in tongues, don't you?" asked Maria. "I wish I had been there. It must have been something to witness!"

"Miraculous." I said with a smile.

I excused myself and went to my bedroom to get my recorder. I was back in minutes, and after a nod of approval from Rune, I turned on the machine.

Rune reached out and took Maria's hand. She looked into his eyes and they smiled. Rune turned his attention to me, and he began.

"It was about 9:00PM and I was sitting in my study, doing homework for my economics class. I thought I heard a noise behind me and I turned to see what it was. Suddenly I saw Maria. She was standing in the bedroom of her apartment. I could see smoke all around her. I could hear fire alarms and sirens in the background, and I knew without question that she was in danger."

"What do you mean 'you saw Maria'?" I asked. "You mean like in a vision?"

"No, not exactly. It was something much more real. I don't know how else to explain it. I looked up, and there she was. But it was more than just seeing her. It was more like *being there* with her. I could see her, hear her. I could feel everything. I could even smell the smoke. I knew in my mind that I was here, in my own home, but I was there as well! I can't explain it any better. Then just as quickly, I was back in my living room. I knew that I had to get to Maria. I didn't know what I could do, I just knew I needed to get to her."

"Did you try to call her first? You know, just to make sure that you were not just imagining this?" I asked.

"No, it didn't even occur to me to call. There wasn't a doubt in my mind as to what I just saw and experienced was real. I knew it was real, and I had to get to her as quickly as possible." He said. "Now here's where it gets a little wired."

"I can hardly wait." I said.

"I dropped everything and headed for the front door. I ran outside, planning to get into my car and drive to Maria's apartment as quickly as possible. She only lives a few kilometers away, and I knew I could get there in a few minutes. Now I know this is hard to believe, and I don't blame you if you don't believe me, but once I stepped outside my door, I found myself instantly standing on the sidewalk just outside Marie's apartment building along with about 20 other people".

"Run that by me again?" I asked.

"One second I am leaving my front door, and the next, I was standing on the sidewalk in front of Maria's apartment building some 3 kilometers away. I can't explain it. I was just there. And, I could see into the building. It was like I could see past the flames, or more to the point, see *through* them. I saw a path through the flames that lead to Maria's apartment. I crossed the fire line, ducking under the security tape placed by the fire department, unnoticed. I heard someone yelling at me to get out of there as I neared the front entrance of the building. Flames and smoke were shooting out from the doorway. Without any hesitation,

I entered the building, which must have looked like I was walking through the flames to those on the outside, but I could see a clear path through the fire and smoke, which lead up the Marie's apartment, which I followed the stairs up to her front door. I opened the door, and went into her bedroom where she was standing, just as I had seen her less than a minute ago from my living room. I took her by the hand and led her out of the building through the same path I followed to get in. It was almost as if the flames and smoke pulled back to allow us to pass."

"All I saw was a wall of flames and smoke." said Maria. "Suddenly Rune was there, and he reached out to me. I took his hand, and he led me through the flames to the outside. I was scared to death. As a matter of fact, I was too scared to speak. It looked like Rune was walking right into the flames, and was taking me with him. I honestly don't know if I followed him because I trusted him, because I had no other choice, or if I was just too confused to realize what I was doing. At any rate, Rune led me out of the building, through the flames and into the street."

"I saw a path through the flames that led to safety," Rune explained, "and I took it. I immediately brought Maria to the paramedics so they could make sure she was all right. I heard someone ask me something, I think they were asking me if I was all right, and the next thing I knew, I was at my front door. It was just like when I left. One second I was one place, the next, someplace else. I wish I could explain it, but I can't."

"Oh my God Maria, were you hurt?" asked Angela.

"No. I was fine, thanks to Rune." She replied. "It was a very frightening experience, and one I will never forget. But I was not hurt. Not a single burn, or smoke inhalation, or anything."

I reached over and turned off the tape. "I can't print any of this." I said

"It's the truth, every word." swore Maria.

"Oh, it's not that I doubt you, Maria. Remember it's me you're talking to. It isn't a question of belief. If I print something like this, every crackpot in the city, every religious fanatic, self-proclaimed psychic, and Holy Roller in the country, will be trying to find you. I imagine that's why you haven't spoken to any other reporters about this, am I right?"

"Absolutely." said Rune. "I called Cardinal Heiss, and we had a long talk about what happened. After consideration to the possible consequences of the publicity, we decided to just let the story fade away, if possible."

"Is that who you called when I arrived earlier this evening?" I asked.

"Yes. I felt he should know I planned to talk to you and that I would be filling you in on everything. He was comfortable with my decision, and trusts my judgment."

"Rune, are you going to tell him everything?" asked Maria.

"There's more?" asked Angela.

"Quite a bit." said Rune. "You see this is just one of several occurrences that have happened to me in the last couple of years. We've managed to keep them quiet since most have happened on Church property."

Chapter 4

"The first incident happened about a year and a half ago, while I was volunteering at St. Eunacious Hospital in Rome. A patient arrived at the emergency room with 3rd degree burns over more than half his body. It was from a car accident that resulted in an explosion. I worked there as a volunteer on the weekends, and was there when the man was brought in. I wanted to offer him spiritual support.

"When I first met the patient, he'd already been medicated pretty heavily, and wrapped in gauze from head to foot. Because of his sedation, it was difficult for him to speak. I felt such pity for the man. I laid my hands on him and prayed. As soon as I touched him, I could feel a burst of heat rising from his body. I didn't think much about it. Most of his body was severely burned after all. I thought the heat I felt was a natural reaction to the burns. The next day, when they removed his bandages to clean and treat the wounds, they discovered his skin was completely intact, with no indication that he had ever been burned at all. It was a complete healing.

"The patient told the doctor that all he could remember was someone laying hands on him and praying. When he awoke the next morning, he felt no pain or discomfort of any kind.

"Honestly, I just prayed for the man, asking God to relieve his suffering. I was not trying to perform a healing or anything like that. I explained to the doctor how I experienced the heat leaving his body when I laid my hands on him, but there was nothing miraculous happening that I was aware of."

"What did Cardinal Heiss say about all this?" I asked.

"He gave orders for everyone at the hospital not to speak of the incident until he had time to talk with the Holy Father. For the most part, everyone obeyed. There were the few whispers here and there of course, that was to be expected. I mean how could you keep something like that a complete secret? Later, the Cardinal lifted the ban on silence, but restricted any discussion about the matter to within the hospital and church walls. I was later summoned to the Vatican for a meeting with the Holy Father. We discussed how I felt about the healing, and what, if any, connections I felt there may have been between that incident and the others."

"Others?" I asked.

"You already know about my speaking in tongues. Through the years, that gift is one I still possess. And then there was another, not too long before the burn patient. A little boy was lost while on a religious retreat with his family. The boy was only five and somehow wandered away from the rest of the family undetected. The retreat was in a deeply wooded area just outside Pirmasens, Germany. "

"I remember that. It was in all the news. We even discussed it in class, and I think one of the students had to do a report on it." I said. "He was missing for about 12 hours I think, and found alive and in good spirits."

"That's right." Rune said. "What nobody knows is *how* he was found."

"You?" I asked.

"Me. It was very much like the fire with Maria. Only that time I was at a bible study with my tutors. I remember we were discussing the trials and tribulations of Job when suddenly I found myself looking at this little boy, lying on the ground next to a swiftly running river's edge. Only I wasn't just looking at him. I was there. At the time, I knew nothing about a missing boy or the search underway to find him. But I saw exactly where he was and knew if the boy was to wake and wander just a few feet, he would fall to his death into the river. Just then I heard one of my instructors call my name, and the vision, if that is what it was, ended as quickly as it came. I was back at the bible study with my tutors. They knew immediately that something had happened and asked if I was all right. I explained what I saw, and that I had to tell someone, or the boy would surely die. But even though I saw him in the woods, I didn't know *where* he was, just that he was near a river and sleeping. I wouldn't be able to explain to someone how to find him.

"One of the tutors instructed me to close my eyes and concentrate on the boy, and I would know what to do. I did as he told me, and almost instantly, like the incident with Maria, I found myself there, standing over the boy. It was like a dream, except I was really there. I picked him up and started to walk. I don't know how long I walked, because time seemed to stand still. Suddenly I was met by several volunteers from a search party, and I handed the boy over to them.

"Everyone focused their attention on the boy, and no one noticed as I turned and walked away. The next thing I knew, I was back with my teachers. I explained to them what happened. I was visibly shaken by the experience.

They tried to calm me down, and explained that I was in a deep state of medi-
tation and prayer, that everything was all right. I knew it was much more than
that. I knew that I was in two places at the same time.

"A short while later we heard the news about the search for a missing boy
who wandered off at a retreat, and was later found and handed over to a group
of volunteers by a rescuer who no one was able to identify.

"Once again, the Church wanted to keep the incident within its walls, and
we were told not to speak of it again."

I glanced at Angela who looked like she had just seen a ghost. I imagine I
looked much the same. "Unbelievable. I don't know what to say, except you
are scaring the hell out me." I said. "Sorry for the use of profanity here, but in
this case, I think it fits. Is there anything else?" I asked.

"Well, there were others, shall I say less dramatic events over the past two
years, but nothing like the last two." said Rune. "I don't know what is happening to me, but whatever it is, it seems to be getting stronger, more intense!"

"Damn!" I said without thinking. "Sorry again!"

Rune looked at me, and I could see the concern in his eyes. I have been
through many things with Rune growing up, and I can honestly say I never
seen him look this worried before.

"To tell you the truth Robert, all this has been pretty unnerving. I am glad
you and Angela are here. I needed a friend to talk to. I just didn't know how
to bring it up. I'm glad I can share this with you both now. Cardinal Heiss
suggested to the Church that these, what he calls 'miracles', be made public.
But I don't look at them as miracles, and I don't want the kind of attention that
would follow such an implication. I trust Cardinal Heiss, but it just doesn't
seem the right thing to do. What bothers me the most is that I don't think it's
over. The 'miracles', I mean. I never know when they will come, or what they
will involve, and lately they involve life and death situations for someone. I
don't know if I can handle it."

"I'm sorry." I said. "Is there anything I can do?"

"Thank you Robert. But this is my problem. I must come to grips with it

"Will you listen to me? For some reason, I have been blessed with special
gifts. Gifts that saves lives, and I call it a problem! God forgive me. But it
would be so much easier if I only knew why this was happening."

Maria leaned forward and took Runes' hands in hers, and looked into his
eyes. "All you can do is trust that whatever is happening to you is God's will.

Whether it is to save lives, or for some greater purpose you don't yet understand, it has all been good. Trust in yourself and your God, who alone knows your true purpose.

"I do, Maria, but I can't help feeling that there is something more."

"What do you mean?" I asked. "Rune, is there something you are not telling us?"

He hung his head. "I don't know. It's complicated. You know I love God and the

Church. And I have complete trust in Cardinal Heiss. He has been a close friend to my family, and to me personally, for as long as I can remember. It is he, that I turn to for guidance, spiritual and otherwise."

"But?" I asked.

"But, I can't help feeling that he is keeping secrets from me, and they are somehow connected to these miracles. He knows more than he is willing to share with me. And it's not just him. There are others as well. "

"Others?" asked Angela. She had been so quiet through all this I almost forgot she was even in the room.

"I mean my teachers, the tutors chosen for me by the Church to help my spiritual growth". Rune grew silent for a moment. "The night I had the 'encounter' with the lost boy, and told them what I saw, what I experienced, well, their response was not exactly what you would expect. I had just told them that out of nowhere, I have a vision of a small boy in great danger, and that I'm transported to somewhere hundreds of miles away for the sole purpose of saving him. Somehow I return, and all without ever leaving the room. They hardly raise an eyebrow, as if this sort of thing happens every day! "

"I see what you mean. That is pretty odd." I said.

"I am not going to print any of this. The story is dead. As far as I am concerned, we never met. I'll tell my professor that I tried, but you were not giving any interviews. He'll huff and puff and I may get a failing grade, but so be it."

"I'm sorry." said Rune. "Maybe we can come up with something you can publish."

"No, it's all right. I say we just forget the paper and school for now. Give Angela and me a little time to digest everything. In the meantime, I want you to know that you are not alone, Rune. I don't know what's happening, but the four of us, working together, will figure it out. But you need to promise me that you will let me know if anything else like this happens. We can't help you if you keep us in the dark. Agreed?"

"Agreed." he said. "I don't know where all this is leading, but knowing that you have my back really takes a lot of the pressure off. I mean it. Thank you. "

"In the meantime, I suggest that we take the next few days to forget all of this and enjoy ourselves." I said. "God knows we can all use a break."

"Great idea." said Angela. "We miss you guys and we don't know when we'll be able to get together again. As of now, it's vacation time. Agreed?"

"Agreed." said Maria with a big smile.

"Agreed." said Rune. "Now what do you say we turn in and get a good night's sleep? We start tomorrow fresh. I have some great ideas for the weekend!"

We had a great vacation, but soon we were back to the same grind of school, work, and research.

We kept in touch of course. There were the occasional weekend get-togethers. We also spent a week together during our summer break. But if Rune was having any more experiences, he kept them to himself. I let him know that Angela and I were there for him if ever he needed us, or just wanted to talk, but I didn't pry. It would have to be his call.

Over the next two years, there would be the occasional story in the newspapers or on local television stations about Rune. The stories were mostly centered on his successes in the business world, guided by his father and new business contacts. It seemed that even before graduating, he was making a name for himself in the financial world. This success was due in large part to his gift for languages. This gift gave Rune the ability to speak fluently in any language, enabling him to interpret even the most subtle meaning of a conversation that escaped the most talented interpreters. That made dealing with foreign bankers effortless for him. It endowed him with an air of authority that instilled confidence with even the most contentious of people. That, combined with his charismatic personality and the influence of his father's reputation, made the name Rune Mikkel synonymous with international banking.

One of the more disturbing stories, at least for me, however, was about a small group of people who claimed to have witnessed Rune performing small miracles, and following him everywhere he went. When questioned, Rune would dismiss the claims as "greatly exaggerated". I wonder!

Chapter 5

In 2008, Rune graduated from KUEI University in Germany two years ahead of time with a PhD in finance. It was a proud day for his father. Shortly after his graduation, Rune made world news by being offered, through the efforts of Cardinal Heiss and his father, an internship with the Vatican Bank in Rome. This in itself was news worthy, but in addition to the internship, he was awarded an honorary ambassadorial role working with financial leaders throughout the world. This was unprecedented in the world of finance.

At the time, the world was in a grip of financial chaos, as many leading banks throughout the world were in collapse or in danger of collapse, including several major banks in the United States. Rune had already made a name for himself, winning the respect and trust of many financial leaders. It was hoped by the Church that Rune would be able to capitalize on his relationship with these leaders. In his role as Financial Ambassador to the Vatican, and with his mastery of language and charismatic personality, the Church believed he could be a guiding force in finding a resolution to the economic crisis. It was a calculated and brilliant move. Under his guidance, the financial situation was defused and, as a result of his efforts, many world banks were spared collapse.

In the meantime, Angela and I continued with our studies, mine in journalism and hers in photography, and kept in touch with Rune and Maria as much as possible.

My relationship with Angela grew with each passing day, and on Christmas Eve of 2008, I proposed marriage. Angela consented to be my wife. We decided it was best to delay the wedding until after graduation. I was surprised at my father's reaction to the news. My father always liked Angela, and my expectation was that he would be overjoyed at the announcement of our engagement. Instead, he appeared to be what I called "cautiously optimistic" at best. Angela's father, on the other hand, was delighted, as was Rune and Maria. Rune, who would be the best man, and Maria the Maid of Honor, wanted the ceremony to be held in Rome, at his parent's estate. I thought that it would be too ostentatious, but he was insistent, and he, with the assistance of Maria, wanted to handle every detail. It would be his wedding present to us.

I couldn't see how he would have the time, but he insisted, and Angela and I finally agreed.

The next year was a blur. Before I knew it, it was graduation day. Both Angela's father and mine attended the ceremony. That was the first time I noticed the tension between the two men. Oh, they were cordial enough, but it was also obvious they were avoiding each other, except when absolutely necessary. I could see that Angela picked up on this as well. That concerned both of us, and we decided that we would have to address it, but not that day. That day belonged to us!

Two weeks after graduation, I had a job offer at a promising newspaper in London, and Angela was considering several options as well. The future looked bright, and we were very excited about moving forward with our wedding plans. That's when the bottom fell out from under us!

It was early Monday morning, one week before I was to begin my new job at the paper. I received an e-mail from Rune, with an air of urgency about it. He needed to see me as soon as possible. He was scheduled to return to his home in Rome the following day, and would set aside time to meet with me if I could get away.I returned his e-mail and told him I would be there as soon as possible. I knew Rune would not ask me to drop everything and go to Rome unless it was very important.

I was waiting outside Angela's apartment when she arrived home from an interview at one of the local news stations. It was one of many that she had sent her resume in hopes of securing a job. She was surprised to see me there, since we were not planning to see each other that night.

"Is everything all right?" she asked as I walked over to meet her.

I wrapped my arms around her and gave her a slow, tender kiss that made my whole being flood with desire. "Everything is fine." I said. "Or I think so, anyway." "Let's go inside, and I'll fill you in." I said.

Angela and I walked to the front door of her apartment, still in a half-hug, my arm around her shoulder, and hers' around my waist. Once inside, I closed the door and turned to face her. I wrapped my arms around her again and looked into her eyes. God she was beautiful! Each time I looked at her, I found something precious I missed before; the way her eyelashes curled, the curve of her lips, the slight dimple on her chin. Each and every discovery added to her beauty. I felt her warmth as she pressed her body against mine. My lips, as if having a mind of their own, found hers. Her lips were warm, sweet, and tender. My heart was pounding in my chest. My entire body responded with shameless presumption to her touch. I had never wanted anyone as much in my entire life! My muscles tightened as her hands began to explore my body, each touch sending wave after wave of titillation. I responded in kind, and could feel her melt in my embrace. Without conscious thought, we found ourselves in her bedroom, having left items of clothing along the way as if marking a trail, now naked and totally committed to our love making.

Much too soon, the morning sun pierced my dreams, waking me to the reality that I would have to leave Angela in a few hours, and didn't want to accept it. But Rune was depending on me, and I promised him I would be there if he needed me.

"Would you like me to go with you?" Angela asked.

"No," I said. "I would love for you to be with me, but I think I should go alone until I know what this is all about." I said. "Do you mind?"

"Of course not. I understand. But call me if you need me." she said.

"Count on it." I said. "I love you! I'll be back as soon as I can."

I held her tight in my arms and kissed her. I knew I would only be gone a few days, but I missed her already. I was not good without her.

I called Rune and informed him that I would catch the next flight out of London and would probably arrive in Rome ahead of him. He told me Maria would meet me at the airport and drive me to his home where I could wait for his return. I told him I could get a room in town, but he insisted I wait for him at his house.

As promised, Maria was waiting for me at the terminal. It was good to see her. She looked as beautiful as ever. After a few pleasantries were exchanged, we left the airport and drove to Runes' house. Once we arrived, Maria led me to the same bedroom I had during my last visit. I asked her if she had any plans for the evening. I wanted to invite her to dinner at the same restaurant Rune treated us to on our last stay, but she said she needed to return home. "Besides," she said, "I think Rune wants to speak to you in private."

"Do you know what time his flight is scheduled to arrive?" I asked.

"He should be arriving around 3:30 this afternoon." she said. "I was hoping that you could drop me off at my apartment, then drive out to the airport and pick him up."

"Of course." I said. "I'm sorry you won't be joining us."

"I think Rune would rather speak to you privately." she said. "But I will see you tomorrow after work. We can visit then."

"I look forward to it." I said. Curiosity was killing me, but I knew better than to press Maria for any more information.

I arrived at the airport about twenty minutes before Rune's flight was scheduled to arrive. It wasn't long before I heard the announcement of the arrival of flight 307 from Frankfurt, Germany. I scanned the passengers as they departed the

aircraft, expecting to see him enter the terminal with his usual light step and smile that put you immediately at ease. Instead, what I saw was a barrage of people circling and working Rune like the paparazzi over a superstar. Rune was answering their questions and giving them instructions as quickly as they could ask. I learned later they were members of his business team, and he was giving them instructions on work assignments to be completed during his stay. It was quite impressive and kind of sad at the same time. This was not the Rune I knew.

It's astonishing how much a person can change in a year. The last time I saw Rune he was much as I had always known him - overtly friendly, comforting, and modest. The Rune I was now seeing was authoritative, commanding, confident, and powerful. It did not change my opinion of him, it was just an observation. Suddenly he noticed me, and waved to me from across the terminal. He gestured to those around him with a slight tilt of his head and focus of his eyes, and without him speaking a word, they left. He walked quickly in my direction, as I made my way across the room to greet him. I could see him smile, and the gentle, gracious man I knew, was back.

It took no time at all and we were back at Rune's home.

"First," he said, "I want to thank you for dropping everything, and coming to Rome at my request. That means a lot to me."

"I told you if you ever needed me, I'd be there, and I meant it. Angela wanted to come as well, but I thought I should come alone."

"I'm glad you did." Rune said. "I'd love to see Angela again, but for the time being, I'd like to keep this just between the two of us."

"That sounds serious." I said. "Is something wrong?"

"I' m sorry if I sound so dramatic. It's just that I have a lot on my plate right now, with this new economic crisis, my duties at the Church, and dealing with my fathers' illness."

"I didn't know your father was ill." I said. "Is it serious?"

"I'm afraid so. We've kept it out of the news, and he's trying to stay strong for Moms' sake, but the truth is, he has very little time left. He was diagnosed with stage 4 pancreatic cancer with metastasis to the liver and kidneys. Last week, they found that the cancer has spread to his brain. I have been helping at home and took over some of Dad's duties at the bank as well."

"Wow! I'm so sorry. What can I do to help?" I asked.

"Thank you for the offer, but I'll be all right. Besides, I asked to see you for an entirely different matter." he said.

"What is it?" I asked.

"I need your help Robert. I want to hire you for a very discreet investigative assignment. It's a very personal and sensitive matter, and it must be kept from the press at all costs."

"You have access to some of the finest investigators in the world. Why not use some of them?" I asked. "I'm barely out of school and have no serious investigative experience worth mentioning. Wouldn't you be better off with someone who has more experience?"

"I have two very good reasons for wanting you." he said. "First and foremost, I must have someone I can trust completely. The trust I have in you is worth more to me than any amount of experience. Second, you already know certain things about me that may come out in an investigation. Things I would like to keep private, at least for now. Besides, don't sell yourself short. What you lack in experience, you more than make up for in honesty and dedication to work and your friends. I would not want anyone but you to handle this, if you are willing. I will pay you well for your time and, of course, cover all expenses."

"The money is not important, you know that. If you need me, then I'm your man." I said.

"That means a lot to me, Robert. But this is first and foremost a job offer. It will take a lot of your time, and you will be paid well for your work. I wouldn't let you do it any other way. I am just thankful that I have you to handle it for me."

"O.K. then," I said, "tell me what you need."

"I need you to investigate me; that is, my past. I need to know who my real parents were, what happened to them, how I came to St. Mary's orphanage, and what connections, if any, did my birth parents have with Cardinal Heiss and my adoptive parents."

"Couldn't you get most of this information yourself?" I asked. "There must be records within the Church and the orphanage."

"No." he replied. "I simply do not have the time. I have made attempts to get at least some of the information, but I have been unsuccessful. Records have disappeared, and people who should have knowledge about my childhood claim to know nothing. I keep running into dead ends. That is why I need the help of a professional, like you."

"Did you ask Cardinal Heiss for help? He must know something or someone that could help you." I asked.

"I did speak with him, but he said he could not help me, since he had no more knowledge about my past than I did." he replied.

"You sound like you doubt him. I always thought you had complete faith in Cardinal Heiss. Do you have any reason to believe he would lie to you or deliberately hold back any information?" I asked.

"No, it's just a feeling I have that he knows something he is unwilling to share."

"Next question." I asked. "Why now? Does this have anything to do with your fathers' condition?"

"No, but that does bring up another point I wanted to talk to you about. If at all possible, I don't want you questioning Dad or Mom about any of this. I don't want them to know about the investigation."

"That closes a lot of very important doors for me." I said. "They should be the first on my list to speak with. They may know a great deal about your parents, and where you come from."

"I realize that, and I'm sorry for tying your hands like this, but I must insist, at least for now".

"I'm sorry if this sounds cold, but considering Mr. Mikkel's health, if he should die, we may lose valuable information I won't be able to get anywhere else."

"I understand." said Rune. "But please..."

"It's your call." I said. "Just so you understand. Is there anything you can give me as a starting point?"

"I know that before I began school, we lived in the Middle East. Cairo, I think. I was very young and we moved a lot due to my fathers' work."

"That's a start. So I'm going to ask again. Why now? I mean with all you are dealing with, why is this so important right now? Isn't this something that should wait a little while until things settle down for you?"

"Without getting into too much detail, one reason is that I am being considered for a very important, very influential position. People from all over the world will be investigating my past; some will be trying to find anything they can to prevent my appointment. I need to know what they might find, starting with my roots. If I am correct, and some secret *is* being kept from me by Cardinal Heiss, I need to know what it is. I must be prepared to defend myself, if necessary." he said.

"If I'm going to have any chance of finding the truth, I am going to need your full cooperation. That means telling me everything you know that will help me. No secrets. Complete disclosure. Are we agreed?" I asked.

"Agreed; no secrets." he said. "If I can help in any way, just let me know. I have some influence that may prove useful, even in Egypt. I will give you a cell phone that will give you direct access to me, and me alone; it's secure. If you need anything, or have anything to report, I want you to use it."

"Anything else you would like to tell me?" I asked.

"Robert, I know I can say this to you and you won't take it the wrong way, like I have some over inflated opinion of myself. But there is something about me that I need to understand. I need to know why I can do things that no one should be able to do. From the time I was a young man, I have been given "gifts" that border on miraculous; speaking in tongues, knowing languages I never studied, seeing visions, being in two places at the same time, controlling people and situations effortlessly. These abilities continue to develop, each new phase stronger and more powerful than the last, and I don't know where they come from, or where it will all end. I need some answers, Robert. I am afraid of losing control of myself. Despite all my abilities, I still need help, and I am depending on you, my closest friend, for that help."

I could see the desperation in his face and my heart nearly broke. "I will do everything I can Rune, I promise. If there are any answers, regardless of the cost, I will find them. You can depend on me."

"I do," he said, "and I am forever grateful."

That night Rune and I dined at his favorite restaurant, and enjoyed each other's company reminiscing of days gone by. We returned home early, well before 10 PM. I called Angela and told her that I would catch an early flight back to London in the morning and would fill her in on what transpired that day. Boy did I miss her!

I told Rune that I would begin my investigation as soon as I got home. I planned to start with St. Mary's Orphanage, even though I expected it to be a dead end, but I didn't want to leave any stone unturned. Next I would take a flight to Egypt and begin searching birth records in the major cities, and birth announcements in the local newspaper archives of some of the larger city libraries.

We said our goodbyes, as Rune expected to be gone before I awoke. Once again, Maria would come by and take me to the airport, despite my insistence that I call a cab.

I woke earlier than expected, and as he said, Rune was already gone. He had a fresh pot of coffee ready for me along with a modest breakfast of muffins and spiced breads with fruits and juice. There was a large manila envelope on the counter addressed to me. It contained a letter in which Rune once again thanked me for taking the assignment, a cell phone with a pre-entered number, a notarized document giving me power of attorney for obtaining documents pertaining to his birth, church, orphanage and school records, along with $10,000 cash to "cover any initial expenses".

Maria arrived around 6:30 am and drove me to the airport. We said our goodbyes and I was on my way home. It hadn't dawned on me before, but it occurred to me later how strange it seemed she never once mentioned my talk with Rune, or even his fathers' illness. Either she already knew why Rune asked to see me, or she didn't want to know.

Chapter 6

The first thing I did when I got home was to call Angela. She was still at work, so we made plans to meet for dinner at a local restaurant. At dinner, I went over my visit with Rune and details of our conversation. I felt a little guilty about telling her, since I never actually told Rune I would share this with Angela, but I believed he must have realize I would be telling her everything.

After dinner, we returned to my place. I had a small one bedroom apartment on the second floor of a fairly new complex. It was small, but comfortable. Angela spent the night, and we made love. I closed my eyes and thanked God for sending me such a wonderful, beautiful woman. I don't know what I did to deserve such a gift. I prayed that I could make her as happy as she made me. I fell asleep with her in my arms.

The next morning I woke before Angela, and quietly slipped out of bed. I took a quick shower, dressed and went to the kitchen to make us breakfast. The smell of perked coffee and sizzling bacon woke Angela. She came staggering into the kitchen still half asleep. Her hair was messed and she was wearing one of my T-shirts, which was long enough to be a nightgown on her. God she looked beautiful!

"Good morning sunshine." I said.

"Good morning love." she replied. "I wanted to be the one making breakfast for you." she said.

"Next time." I said. "Today it's on me."

"You're sweet. No wonder I love you so much." She walked over to me and gave me a kiss. I almost dropped her plate. We both sat down and began breakfast.

"I was giving your assignment some thought." she said. "I know you told me that Rune said there were no records of his birth or parent's names at the orphanage or church, but what about the school? Don't they require information like date and place of birth when you enroll a child? Maybe they would have a copy of Rune's birth certificate, or Baptismal record. They should have the name of Rune's parents. And what about Rune's birth certificate. He must have one."

"Yes, he has one," I said, "but it lists the Mikkel's as his parents, and birthplace as Frankfurt, Germany. We already know that is not correct. It was the address of his adoptive parents that was used. But as for the school, Rune didn't mention checking with them, although I believe he must have. I planned on checking it out anyway."

"And what about this?" asked Angela. "You mentioned the Mikkel family traveled a lot while Rune was very young. Wouldn't he have to have a passport?"

"I suppose so." I said. "But even if he had one, it would just list Mr. and Mrs. Mikkel as his legal parents. It wouldn't give the names of his birth parents."

"I know," she said, "but to get the passport, wouldn't they need records of when and where he was born? Maybe they would have the real address of his birth on them."

"Smart." I said. "It's worth a try, I'll check it out. You know, you could be a great help to me on this."

"I wish I could, I start my new job this morning, and I hate to quit before I even begin. It would look bad on my resume."

"I know you're right. I guess I'm just being selfish." I said.

"You just keep on being selfish, especially when it comes to me. I love it!" she said.

I leaned over and gave her a loving kiss. "Don't start something you can't finish." she said as she pushed us apart. "I have to be at work in thirty minutes."

"You're right again. I have a lot to do myself. I guess I'll start with phone calls, and see if I get lucky. I'll call you at noon if that's all right." I asked.

"You better." she said.

That morning I was able to contact both the orphanage and the elementary school Rune and I attended. I made an appointment to see the Director of Records at the orphanage for 10 am the next morning, and one with the school at 3:45pm the same day. It would be tight, but I was sure I would be able to manage both. I was also able to get the phone number for the department head in the passport office in Cairo, Egypt. I had no idea if this was the same office Mr. Mikkel would have applied for a passport for Rune, but was hoping that I would at the least get some information on how to obtain the records and documents filed with an application. This is the part of any investigation that is more like a scavenger hunt. Only once you have several pieces, can you begin to put the puzzle together. It's the discovery and collection of those pieces that is the true challenge and test of an investigator.

The next morning I was able to catch the 5:00 AM flight out of Heathrow and was in Rome by 8:30, plenty of time for my 10:00 AM appointment. I was greeted by Sister Mary Clarence, head of the records department at the *Collegio Piccoli amici di Gcau Home For Young Boys*. She had been working at that facility for over thirty years and remembered when Rune was brought in. She told me she spoke with Rune only a few weeks prior, and that he, too, was seeking the records of his admission.

I informed her that I was aware of his visit, and was there at his request. It was my hope to discover the names of his true birth parents. I explained that since they were both deceased, I understood that information would be accessible to him.

"I explained to Rune that it is customary to retain records of admission for only ten years after the placement of our boys, the records are then archived on microfiche and held at our satellite office in Rome. However, such records rarely, if ever, contain the name of the parents. It is for their protection, you understand." she explained.

"Yes." I said. "However, since Runes' parents were killed in a car crash, and he was not put into an orphanage because of abandonment by either of his parents, isn't it possible the records may contain that information, or at least give a place of birth?"

"Yes, that would be true *if* Rune's parents died in a car crash, but that was not the case. I was here when Rune was brought to Collegio Piccoli. I remember clearly that he was an abandoned child." she said.

"Are you certain about that?" I asked?

"Absolutely. I remember because it was such an unusual case." she said.

"How was it unusual?" I asked?

"Yes, because he was brought in by a Bishop. That was the first and only time I have ever admitted an infant that was in the custody of a Bishop."

"Do you remember the name of the Bishop, Sister?" I asked?

"Of course I do. I have been following his career ever since. Are you Catholic Mr. Claiborne?" she asked?

"Yes Sister, I am." I replied.

"Well then I am sure you have heard of him." she said. "He is Cardinal Heiss. Of course he was Bishop Heiss back then. I was told that back then, Bishop Heiss worked at the Vatican. I believe he had a position of some importance with the Vatican Bank."

"Did you tell Rune this when he was here?" I asked.

"No, we did not discuss that. He simply wanted a copy of the records of his admission to the orphanage, and when I explained we did not have them here, he simple thanked me for my time and left."

I was stunned, but tried not to show it.

"Sister!" I heard a loud voice from behind me shout. I turned quickly and saw on older priest standing only a few yards away. I wondered how long he had been there and if he overheard our conversation. By the look on Sister Clarence's face, I could tell she also had been unaware of his presence.

"May I speak with you in private please?" His tone was unmistakably angry.

"Yes Father." she replied.

"Excuse us." he said as he led Sister Clarence away with his hand on her shoulder.

It was obvious my meeting had come to an end, but not before I learned something. Cardinal Heiss was indeed keeping secrets from Rune. But why was it so important to keep the identity of his parents secret, that he would lie about it?

This was incredible information, and it was only the first day of the investigation! I planned on talking to Sister Clarence again if I could get her away from that priest. I thought maybe a phone call would be best. I would try that later this evening, once I got home.

Next I was on my way to my old elementary school. To tell the truth, I was anxious to see the place again. I enjoyed my time there, with a few exceptions of course, and wondered if any of the teachers Rune and I had still worked there. I was pleased to see that a few did. One of my favorite teachers, Ms. Chaplin (some say she was related to the famous Charlie Chaplin, but I never knew for sure) was still teaching English to the fifth grade. She remembered me and Rune. Not many who met him ever forgot him. She invited me into her office and we had a pleasant talk. She asked what I chose to do with my life, and I told her I graduated from the University of London with a Masters in journalism, and was working as an investigative reporter with a local paper. She seemed impressed.

"And what about Rune?" she asked. "Are you two still thick as thieves?"

"Rune and I have kept in touch, and see each other as often as time allows." I said. "As a matter of fact, it's Rune that brings me here today."

"How so?" she asked.

"A simple matter, really." I said. "I am here to retrieve a copy of his school records for him."

"Couldn't he have done that himself with a phone call or by mail?" She asked.

"I suppose so," I said, "but I was in the area on other business anyway, so I offered to stop by for him." I hated lying to her, but I wanted to keep my business from anyone who did not have a need to know.

"You will have to go to the records department, but I am not sure how long they keep those records. Do you know where the office is?" she asked.

"Yes I do, thank you. I was headed that way just before I spotted you. I have an appointment with Mr. Wallace at 3:45. I just wanted to say hello first".

She smiled and thanked me for taking the time to see her and wished both Rune and myself good fortune and good health. "Now, if your meeting with Mr. Wallace is for 3:45, you better hurry. Mr. Wallace hates tardiness." she said.

I thanked her for the heads-up on Mr. Wallace, and quickly made my way to the records office. I found Mr. Wallace glancing at his watch when I walked in.

"I thought maybe you weren't coming." he said.

"I'm sorry." I said". I ran into one of the teachers I had when I was here as a student, and felt it would be rude if I didn't stop to say hello."

"Touching." he said without a smile. "I would have thought it ruder to keep someone waiting."

"The reason I am here," I explained, "is that Rune Mikkel hired me to investigate the circumstances involving his placement at the *Collegio Piccoli amici di Gcau Home For Young Boys,* subsequent adoption by Mr. And Mrs. Mikkel, and enrollment here at Saint Francis."

"I don't see how I can help you." he said.

"It is his hope, that despite the fact the required documents for admission to Saint Francis would list the Mikkels as his legally adoptive parents, it is possible that they may also have provided his true birthplace, and gives Rune a place of origin to begin his quest." I explained.

"Even if that were true, I have no authority to hand over confidential information to you on just your word." He said.

I opened my briefcase, and handed him the power of attorney signed by Rune and sealed by the Magistrate of Rome. He read the document, folded it up and returned it to me.

"I will need time to locate the paperwork, if indeed, it is still here."

"No problem." I said. I will be glad to come back tomorrow, say around 4:00 PM?" I asked?

"I have obligations and commitments to the orphanage that require my attention. I doubt that I will have time to meet with you tomorrow, or any day during the week. I will contact you as soon as I have something for you."

"Thank you Mr. Wallace." I said. "I look forward to hearing from you in the near future." He did not reply. I left his office feeling like I just tried to rob a local bank. I could not understand his reluctance to assist me. If he was a past teacher of mine that I pissed off, I would understand, but I had never met this man before. And his attitude today was completely opposite of the phone conversation we had the day before. Did someone talk to him and persuade him not to cooperate with me, and if so, who, and more importantly, why? Maybe I was just being paranoid. After all, no one knew about my business with Rune except Angela, Maria and, of course, Rune.

It was after 10:00pm before I got back to London. It was a long and frustrating day. I decided it was too late to try and reach Sister Clarence, but intended to make that call a priority first thing in the morning. I called Angela to let her know I was home, and made plans for an early lunch. I told her I would fill her in on the days' events then. I was glad to hit the pillows and was out like a light in a matter of minutes.

The next morning, true to my word, my first order of business after breakfast was to call the orphanage in Rome and ask to speak to Sister Clarence.

"I'm sorry." said the woman who answered the call. "Sister Clarence is no longer with us. She passed away late last night."

For a moment I was speechless. "What do you mean she passed away last night? I saw her yesterday morning, and she was fine. What happened? Was it an accident?" I asked.

"Sister Clarence suffered from poor health for a long time." she said. "She had a heart condition that required a pace-maker for several years now."

"Half the people I know have pacemakers." I said. "I don't expect to hear that they died overnight because of it!"

"Yes, I understand your grief. Nonetheless, Sister Clarence is gone. I'm sorry. Is there someone else you would like to speak to?" she asked.

I was silent for a moment. It was taking time to register what happened. "Could you give me the name and number of her closest living relative?" I asked. "I would like to give my condolences."

"Sister Clarence had no family other than the Church. But we appreciate your sympathy. If you wish, you could make a contribution in her name to the orphanage. I am sure she would have appreciated that." she said.

How cold, I thought. "I'll do that, thank you." I said abruptly, and hung up. What was happening? My stomach was getting sick, and I didn't like what I was thinking.

I met with Angela around 11:00 AM for lunch as planned. It was good to see her. She immediately made my day better, and lifted my spirits. She noticed, nonetheless, that something was bothering me. I didn't want to alarm her, so I chose my words carefully as I explained my visits to the orphanage and my meeting with Mr. Wallace. Then I told her about my phone call that morning and the news of Sister Clarence's death.

"Oh my God Robert, what is going on?" she asked.

"I'm not sure." I said. "This investigation is becoming much more complicated than I thought it would."

"Are you going to tell Rune about this?" she asked.

"Not yet. I am not sure what, if anything, it all means. I need more answers. Right now all I have are questions. Besides, what would I say; I got nowhere with the orphanage or school, and by the way, one of the Sisters at the orphanage died after talking to me?"

"You might mention what you learned about Cardinal Heiss." she said. "He is one of the concerns Rune has, isn't he?"

She made a good point, but I still felt I should wait until I had more information.

As my investigation for Rune continued, the worlds' financial crisis continued to grow. Ireland, Portugal, Greece and Spain had already gone bankrupt, while France, Italy, Japan and even the United States, the largest debtor nation in the world, following close behind. If the U.S. should collapse financially, the rest of the world would follow. This angered many of the European nations who accused the United States of greed and mismanagement of funds. Distrust, finger pointing, even threats of war were rampant. In the middle of all this was Rune. Due to his great popularity with many of the world leaders, and his uncanny ability with language, he was thought to be, by many, the most trusted man in the world right about then. It was no surprise when the Vatican, for a second time, offered his services as Ambassador to oversee a United Nations Emergency Summit to deal with the crisis.

In an unprecedented move, all the other interpreters were dismissed from the Summit. It was decided that Runes' gift of tongues provided a level of pure language, unequaled by any individual interpreter. There were complaints, mostly from those who never had the opportunity to work with Rune, though most knew of his reputation and legendary gift of tongues. It did not take long before their misapprehension melted away and was replaced with sheer amazement.   It was said that each banking representative of every nation was able to express, through Rune, their thoughts, concerns, needs and wants without the baggage of emotion or misspoken words, and the receivers of the messages were able to accept a level of understanding never before realized, due to the efforts and gifts of Rune.   As each nation represented was given a chance to speak, Rune interpreted his or her words to the entire assemble at one time, each hearing him in their own individual language and dialect. That saved a considerable amount of time, allowing the assembly to accomplish their goals with unprecedented speed. It was a complete success. It was like each person was able to read the mind and heart of every person there.   Resolutions were quickly agreed upon, and for the first time in decades, there was a sense of hope for the world once again.   And all the credit was given to Rune. The story was carried on every major news station and paper in the world. It was hailed as a "Modern Day Miracle of Biblical Proportions".

Rune was thrust from the shadows forever that day. A new Rune John Paul Mikkel was emerging – a strong, powerful man with a loyal following of some of the most influential men and women in the world.   By the end of the month, Rune was elected President of the Vatican Bank.   Nothing would ever be the same for him again, or me, for that matter!

Chapter 7

It was during that emergency summit meeting when Rune's adoptive father died. Despite everything that Rune's father had accomplished in his very successful career, his death seemed newsworthy only because of his relationship to Rune. I was in Egypt at the time,   trying to locate anyone that might remember something about Runes birth, or the death of his parents. I called Rune to express my sympathy, and told him that I planned to return to Germany for the funeral. He informed me however, there would be no need. It was his father's wishes that when the time came, he did not want to be put on display, like a mounted fish on the wall. "We all die" Mr. Mikkel told Rune before his death. "It's going to be painful enough for your mother. All I want is a small service at home, no showing, and burial in the family cemetery. " Rune was going to honor that request.

I understood, in a way, so I remained in Egypt and decided to focus my search in Cairo but was getting nowhere in my attempt to locate any living person that may have knowledge about Rune's birth or his parents. No one could remember anything about a deadly car crash around the time of Runes' birth. I decided to visit the local library and search the archived newspapers as a last resort. It would be a long and tedious task.

While scanning through one of the more popular local papers dated around Rune's birthday, something caught my eye! It had nothing to do with Rune or any accident. It was a follow-up story about an unsolved murder case, involving the death of several tomb robbers that occurred a few years prior to Runes' birth. The story focused on an interview with an investigator that, at the time, was thought to have some connection to the crime. It was the investigator's name that made my heart do a summersault in my chest. His name was *James Claiborne*; My father!

In all my years, listening to all the many stories of his adventures, my father never mentioned anything about this to me. A quick search of the records disclosed the original coverage of the event. It was a fascinating story about a multiple murder case that went unsolved. I wondered why my father never told me about it. Especially now that he knew I was traveling to Egypt, to the very city in which my own father obviously visited, and during the very time period I was investigating. I would have many questions about this when I returned home.

I made a copy of all the articles I could find involving the case. Then I went to the local police station to see if I could get any first-hand information about the story. As it turned out, the head of the Department of Justice worked as a young policeman at the time, and was part of the initial recovery team of the bodies found at the site. I asked if he knew anything about the investigator alleged to have some connection to the crime. He remembered that an investigator was working for the lead architect of the crime, Dr. Mark Osborne, on what he claimed was an unrelated case. It was unclear how much, if anything, the investigator may have known about the theft and murders; he was never formally charged due to lack of evidence. I doubt the man I spoke with made any connection between my name and the name of the investigator of whom I was questioning. At least he never made any indication that he did.

I wrapped up my work and took the next flight out of Cairo back to London. I was very anxious to speak to my father, although I knew that it would have to wait for a while. My father was out of the country, visiting an old friend in the United States, and what we needed to talk about could not be done by phone. I called Angela, but just got her voice mail. I left a message giving her my flight information, and told her there was an unexpected twist in the investigation.

I was so glad to finally get home. I called Angela again. This time she answered. I asked if she had some available time, because there was something I wanted to talk to her about. She suggested I come over. It would give a chance to shower and change, since she just got in from work. I told her I would pick-up dinner on the way, and we could eat while we talked. I arrived at Angela's around 7P.M. As we sat down for dinner, I filled her in on my visit to Egypt, and what I learned about my fathers' work with Dr. Mark Osborne. "Why would he not tell me he was in Cairo, and a person of interest in a murder investigation?" I asked.

"Maybe it was something he wanted to forget. Or maybe he was embarrassed to mention he worked for a tomb robber and murderer." she said.

"Still," I said, "not to mention anything about being there, or about his working for Dr. Osborne or being questioned by the police about his possible involvement in a criminal case. It just doesn't seem right that he would keep it from me. My gut tells me there is more to this."

"When do you expect him home?" Angela asked.

"He should arrive sometime tomorrow evening. I'll give him a day before I hit him with this. Give him a chance to unwind from his trip. Would you like to come with me when I go to see him?" I asked.

"Maybe this is something you should discuss with your father privately. If there is anything he isn't telling you, my being there might make it more difficult for him." she said.

"You're right. I'll see him alone. Have I told you how much I love you lately?" I asked.

"Not for almost an hour now." she answered.

"It's Long overdue." I said. With that I pulled her to me and gave her a warm, loving kiss. "Can you spend the night?" she asked.

"Just try and send me away!" I said.

The next morning was Saturday, and neither Angela nor I had to rush off to work so we decided to sleep in. When we finally got the ambition to get up, I made brunch and we sat in the living room watching the news on TV. The news was not good. Things were heating up in the Middle East over the past few months, and no one was predicting a good outcome.

It had not even been a month since Rune single handedly averted a world-wide financial collapse, and was promoted to President of the Vatican Bank. Now that ugly monster was raising its head again. It seemed that without Runes' constant guidance, nations could not find a way to work together to sequel the tide of discontent. This time it was not just due to the economy, although many put the blame there. Nations in the Middle East were rapidly achieving nuclear capability. North Korea was taking on a whole new aggressive stance against the West. Increase in natural disasters exhausted resources from countries all over the globe, to include the United States which was hit with record breaking tornadoes, hurricanes, earthquakes, floods and drought in the past year. It would appear that all of Rune's hard work was about to be for naught. A strong hand was needed, and more and more, the people were turning to Rune. Hardly a day went by without seeing his name or face on Cable News, the internet, and local papers all around the world.

The most imminent threat the world was facing at the moment was the nuclear proliferation of Iran and North Korean, which was something that neither the United States nor Israel was willing to allow. The morning news was focused on threats of a pre-emptive strike on both countries by the United States,

Israel and Great Britain. Tensions reached a new height throughout the world, and many world leaders were calling for another emergency United Nations Summit, demanding it be led by none other than Rune himself. The hope being, that with his gift of tongues, he could repeat the success accomplished at the last summit, no matter how short lived it was. Some believed that he may be their last hope to avoid an all-out nuclear war.

"Talk about having the weight of the world on your shoulders." I said. "I wonder how Rune is handling all this."

"Well, he does have a good support system, with the Church, Cardinal Heiss, his fathers' associates, and of course you." said Angela

"And you." I said. "But still. What do they want from the guy? He pulled them out of the fire once already. How much can one man do?"

"You have your hands pretty full yourself, working for Rune. Are you going to see your father tonight and find out about that business in Egypt?"

"Yes." I said. "I don't look forward to it either I might add. My dad never hid anything from me before. I'm not sure I want to know why he did about this."

We continued to watch the news in silence, but I could not keep my mind off my dad.

My dad was in a great mood when I arrived. His trip to the United States was one he looked forward to for a long time. I could tell that he was anxious to tell me all about it. I planned to listen, pretend to be interested, before I broached the topic of Egypt. That didn't work. He could tell almost immediately that something was wrong.

"What's wrong son?" he asked. "Is everything o.k. between you and Angela?"

"It's nothing like that dad." I said. There was a few seconds of silence. "I told you that I am working a case for Rune. Well, I was in Cairo a couple of days ago. I went to the public records department at City Hall, and the public library to do some research for the case. When I was searching the library archives for a specific story, I accidentally came across an article about an interview with an investigator suspected in the murder of a group of tomb robbers."

"It was me, wasn't it?" he asked. "You found the article about me being questioned in connection with the case. I'm sure you read that although they found no connection between me and the crimes committed, they felt that I knew more than I was telling. When they were unable to pin anything on me, I was released and told to leave the country".

"It said that you knew, and was working for, one of the men murdered. Is that true?"

"Yes." he said. "But I did not have anything to do with the murder of those men, or the theft of any artifacts."

"Why did you keep this a secret from me all these years dad? Did you think I wouldn't believe you?"

"I wanted to protect you." he said.

"Protect me from what?" I asked.

"It's a long story," he said, "and one I hoped I would never have to tell. But before I begin, you need to call Angela and ask her to come over, and bring her father with her."

"Mr. Shelton? What does he have to do with this?" I asked.

"I will explain everything once Angela and her father get here. In the meantime, there is something I need to do, so make yourself a drink, and try to be patient. It's going to be a long night." he said. He got up, took his keys from the hook by the door where he always put them, and left. I just stood there in disbelief. My father never kept secrets from me before. I began to wonder how well I knew the man I called dad.

Chapter 8

Dad got back about 10 minutes after Angela and her father arrived, and he was carrying a large, weather worn briefcase. Mr. Shelton didn't seem exactly happy to see dad, and I didn't think it was because he was summoned here at this late hour. Whatever my dad was going to tell us, I was sure Mr. Shelton already knew. My father invited us to get comfortable (as if that was possible), and once we were settled, he began.

"About thirty years ago, Mr. Shelton and I worked together on a case for Dr. Osborne, who was a young archeologist with a promising future. I was hired as an investigator, and Mr. Shelton worked as my photographer. Dr. Osborne hired me to uncover the identity of the person or persons who contracted with him along with an anthropologist, Dr. Hilterman, to conduct a secret and illegal archeological dig in Cairo."

"Why would any archeologist want to conduct an illegal dig anywhere, especially in Cairo?" I asked.

"Good question." my father said. "I'm sure the money was a motivating factor, but I suspect it was more than that. Every archeologist in the world had been trying to get permission for a dig in that region for decades, but as you probably know, the Egyptian government had, and still does today, forbid any excavations on the Giza Plateau to anyone. It was a chance of a lifetime, and my guess is that it was too great of an opportunity to pass up, regardless of the risks. At any rate, Dr. Osborne agreed to do the dig. However, it bothered him that he never knew the name of the people financing the project and giving the orders. All the details were handled through a third party and financing was conducted through a Swiss bank account. What made the dig even more curious was that neither Dr. Osborne nor his partner, Dr. Hilterman, was ever told exactly what they were expected to find."

"That doesn't make any sense." I said.

"Exactly." said my father. "That's where I came in. I was hired by Dr. Osborne to find out anything I could about the benefactor(s). He gave me what little information he had. I approached Mr. Shelton and hired him to assist me as photographer."

"Why my father?" asked Angela.

"We knew each other. Actually, we worked together on several cases in the past. I trusted your father, and knew he did excellent work. He was the logical choice." my father said.

At this point I already had a hundred questions, but decided to let my father tell the story in his own way. Any questions would wait until later.

"The investigation became more involved than I could have ever imagined, taking us to several countries throughout Europe, and eventually into Egypt. Soon into the investigation, we found ourselves mixed up with one of the most secretive and dangerous cults on earth. We were over our heads, submerged in mystery, espionage, betrayals, and even murder. Our investigation led us into the very heart of *The Illuminate!*"

The Illuminate! I have heard about them, as did Angela. Powerful, fearless and stealth, born out of the Catholic Church, centuries old. Some say they were just a legend, a fantasy of some twisted mind. Others swear to their existence, and claim firsthand knowledge of their involvement in many world changing events; some for good, some not so good. But whether real or imagined, the name itself conjured up fear in the minds of those who knew of them.

"We swore never to talk about this to anyone." said Mr. Shelton. The look on his face was more of fear than anger.

"I don't think we have a choice, Michael. Robert and Angela need to have all the facts. We can't protect them if they don't know the whole story. You know as well as anyone how dangerous this is. It could mean the difference between life and death!" my father said.

"A matter of life and death? Who's life and death?" I demanded. I was starting to get a little alarmed. Angela reached over and took my arm.

"Yours." my father said. "But maybe it doesn't have to be that way."

"Are you sure about this James?" asked Angela's father?

"I don't see that we have any choice Mike, do you?" he asked.

"Very well then, but we'll have to tell them everything. Agreed?" asked Mr. Shelton.

Angela and I exchanged stares. "What the hell is going on?" I asked?

My father reached for the briefcase, and opened the lock that secured it.

"I'm sorry." said Mr. Shelton. "Maybe we should have told you both about this a long time ago, but we felt that it was best to try and keep you in the dark, hoping that you would never need to know the truth." Looking at me, he continued. "When you first met Rune all those years ago in elementary school, we never thought you would develop such a strong and lasting relationship. If we did, your father would probably have taken you out of that school and moved to another location far from him. But as time passed and he saw how close you two became, he decided it might be best to pretend ignorance. Then there was that business with the confirmation and Rune's special gift occurred. Your father called me and we had a meeting. We discussed our options, and once again decided that doing nothing was probably the best option. I see now that we made a terrible mistake. Then you met Angela, and fell in love. I don't know if that was irony or fate. Either way, it seems that you are both heading into something that neither of you are prepared for."

"My investigation began by trying to locate and identify the man who approached my client with the offer to conduct the dig." my father said. "It didn't take long before I was able to identify him as Charles Schmitt, from Frankfurt, Germany. I discovered that little information about Mr. Schmitt was available. I was, however, able to put a wiretap on his phone. It turned out that he was making a number of calls to someone located within Vatican City, but the person on the other end of the call was never identified, due to their strict security. There was another number I was able to trace, however, and that was a number listed to someone in in the United States Air Force. His name was Colonel Cornel Wiseman. After a little research, I discovered that Colonel Wiseman was the Deputy Commander for the Stealth Satellite Strategic Command Center located in Central Europe. Earlier that same year, Colonel Wiseman resigned from military duty under a cloud of suspicion, and retired to an island off of Central America."

"What was he suspected of?" I asked.

"Some secret files were found missing from the SSSCC. It was suspected that Colonel Wiseman was responsible for their disappearance. After a full investigation, not enough evidence was found to officially charge him of the crime. He resigned his commission and took early retirement."

"Did you ever discover what were in the files that disappeared?" I asked?

"That was classified information," said my father, "however, I had a connection from my time in the military, who was working for the Secret Service. Through him, I was able to discover the files contained, among other things, a satellite image of a chamber, deep under the foot of the Great Sphinx in the Giza Plateau. It appeared to hold no military significance, so was filed away for future reference. It appeared to have no real value to anyone. That's why the theft made no sense."

"Well it obviously was of value to someone." I said.

"It was at that point I brought your father into the investigation. I needed pictures, and he would be my photographer. He was able to get photos of both Charles Schmitt and Colonel Wiseman, which I entered in my report for Dr. Osborne. In one of the candid photos of Charles Schmitt, he was meeting with another unknown man, who appeared to be a priest." He reached into the box and pulled out a folder. Inside was a photo that he handed to me. "This man is Charles Schmitt." my father said as he pointed to one of the men in the photo.

But, do you recognize the priest?" he asked.

At first I didn't make the connection. Then I saw it! The other man, the priest shaking Charles Schmitt's hand was a very young Cardinal Heiss.

"Isn't that---?" Angela started to asked.

"Yes." I said. "That's Cardinal Heiss".

"Well, Father Heiss at the time. He was a priest working at the Vatican Bank, in Rome." My father said. "I didn't know if his meeting with Charles Schmitt had any connection with the case, but thought it warranted further investigation. I kept a close watch on them both for the next several weeks. The only people Mr. Schmitt seemed to have any contact with was Father Heiss, my client Dr. Osborne, and, Dr. Fronz Hilterman, a Forensic Anthropologist. It was almost impossible to get background information on either man. I began to suspect that the name

Charles Schmitt was an alias. Father Heiss proved just as difficult. Although I was

able to ascertain his work at Vatican Bank and residence in Vatican City, all other information was not forthcoming. I did suspect, however, that he was the person on the other end of Mr. Schmitt's calls to Vatican City, but was never able to prove it. Father Heiss was seen, however, on one occasion meeting with a man I later identified, thanks to the good work of Angela's father, as Hoberto Calvine."

Once again my father handed me a photo taken from the folder, which identified Mr. Calvine. "It turns out that Mr. Calvine was the Director of the Banco Ambrosiano in Italy. I was later able to make a more substantial connection between Mr. Calvine, Father Heiss and Colonel Wiseman."

"Holy shit!" I said. "Sorry dad."

"There is more." he said. "Mr. Calvine was under suspicion of fraud and embezzlement of funds from the Banco Ambrosiano of more than three billion dollars. Your priest, Father Heiss, certainly hung out with some pretty shifty people." He said.

"Not *my* priest." I said. "But he and Rune certainly have a close relationship."

"Closer than you may think." my father answered. "Mr. Calvine was arrested and put in jail, pending trail. He was represented by one of the top criminal attorneys in Italy, paid for by Mr. Rolf Mikkel."

"Runes' father?" I asked.

"Yes." said Angela's father.

"It gets better." my father said. "On a hunch, I decided to do an extensive investigation into Fronz Hilterman."

"Dr. Osborne's' partner?" I asked.

"Yes. I told myself I was just being thorough, but to tell you the truth, I had a hunch something was up with that man. I never informed Dr. Osborne about investigating his partner. That way, if Dr. Hilterman found out about my spying on him, he could claim "plausible deniability", and be truthful about it. As it turned out, Dr. Hilterman was making routine calls to the *Swiss Bank Corporation* in Basel, Switzerland. It was at this point I realized I needed additional help, so I contacted a very good friend of mine. His name was Mino Pecorelli, a well-known and respected investigative journalist who often worked on cases involving the Vatican. Although I hadn't seen Mino for several years, he and I collaborated on many cases in the past, and had mutual respect for each other's work. I contacted him and explained my situation. He asked me to send him everything I had so far, and he would see what he could do.

"It was about two weeks after I sent him my notes and the photos Mr. Shelton had taken, when I received a call, asking me to meet him at a coffee shop just outside Geneva, Switzerland. I thought that was a strange place to meet, but didn't question him. I was sure he had a good reason to choose such a secluded place. We agreed to meet the next day around 9:30AM. I arrived early, and found Mino already there. Despite being a cold and cloudy day, we sat outside at Mino's request. He explained that it would be safer talking outside, because there would be less chance of being overheard. I asked him what he discovered. I wasn't prepared for his answer."

"For the last two years," Mino said, "I have been working in collaboration with the Direzione Investigativa Antimafia (DIA), which is a joint organization of Polizia di Stato, Carabinieri and Guardia di Finanza for the fight against organized crime in Italy. I have been trying to collect information on several high profile bankers and business men, suspected of laundering money for the Mafia as well as other underground organizations throughout Europe and the United States. It took a long time and substantial risk on my part, but I managed to gain the trust of a few men high in those organizations. From what I have been able to uncover so far, the scope of their operations extend much further than previously believed by the DIA, to include extortion, kidnapping, murder and terrorism. They are a ruthless bunch, capable of almost anything."

"I explained," said my father, "that I found his story very intriguing, but I didn't see what that had to do with *my* investigation. He told me to let him finish. I apologized and let him continue."

"At first, I was reluctant to accept your request for assistance with your case," said Mino, "due to the extent of my involvement with my own investigation, until I looked at the photographs you sent me. There were two, in particular, that caught my attention."

"After a slow, but deliberate scan of the area," said my father, "Mino took two photos from an inside pocket of his overcoat. He slid the photos across the table to me, face down. I picked them up and looked at them. They were the photos of Hoberto Calvine, Director of the Banco Ambrosiano in Italy, and Dr. Fronz Hilterman."

"This is not the first time I've seen these men." Mino told my father. "I have seen them both associating with men I know to be part of the organizations I am investigating. I am certain of their involvement with activities involving those organizations. How deeply they are involved, I am not sure. Mr. Calvine is presently under arrest and awaiting trial for embezzlement of funds from the Banco Ambrosiano."

"I heard about that." my dad told him.

"James, these are dangerous men." said Mino. "So far, your involvement with them is minimal. You need to give some serious consideration to the possible consequences if you decide to continue with your investigation."

"I accepted my assignment knowing there would be risks." my dad told him. "I have never backed out of a job because of the possible danger it posed, and I am not about to start now."

"I understand." said Mino. "I expected nothing less of you. So, if you are determined to go forward, I am willing to help you all I can. But I have a favor of my own to ask of you. You know that I recently lost Ruth to breast cancer. We have a beautiful baby girl, and now I find myself a single parent. She depends on me for everything. If, God forbid, something should happen to me, I need to know that she will be taken care of. I couldn't bear the thought of her being put in an orphanage. I know it is lot to ask, but if something should happen, promise me that you will see she is taken care of."

"I explained to him that I had a son of my own, and I knew exactly how he felt." said dad. "I promised that I would, if the time came, see to it his daughter would be taken care of, and he shouldn't worry.

"I heard from Mino several times over the next month." my father said, "and each time he gave me information regarding Mr. Calvine and Dr. Hilterman, as well as information regarding his *own* investigation with the *DIA*. Although he never said it, I suspected that he believed there was a connection between his investigation and mine. But what possible connection could there be with an archeological dig in Egypt, the Mafia, the Vatican and the president of the Banco Ambrosiano ?"

Chapter 9

"While Mino was focusing on our European friends, I turned my attention to Colonel Cornel Wiseman." my dad said. "As I already mentioned, I still had connections with the Secret Service, and through them, I was able to discover some little known facts about the Colonel.

"Colonel Wiseman grew up in a small town outside Maryland, USA. His family migrated to the U.S. from Scotland sometime in the 17th century. His father, like his grandfather before him, were Freemasons; his grandfather achieved the prestigious 14th degree: *Scottish Knight of Perfection*. Although it was unclear what degree his father held, it was rumored he ascended to the 30th degree: *Grand Elected Knight Kadosh* (also known as the "Knight of the Black and White Eagle"). At first, this fact, although interesting, did not seem important to me. But then I remembered something I read in one of the reports Mino sent me on Hoberto Calvine. He, too, was a Freemason! On a hunch, I asked Mino if he knew if any of the other men he was investigating were Freemasons. His results were quite enlightening. There were more men than I would have imagined on his list, but among those he was able to verify as Freemasons that were of interest to me included:

Colonel Wiseman

Dr. Fronz Hilterman

Hoberto Calvine

Michele Sindona (Alias Charles Schmitt)

Father Paul Heiss"

"Couldn't that just be a coincidence?" I asked? "After all, there are millions of Freemasons throughout Europe, isn't there"?

"Well," my dad said, "here is another coincidence for you. They all belong to the same lodge. *The Lodge of Edinburgh No. 1,* in Edinburgh, Scotland, also known as Mary's Chapel. It is one of the oldest orders in the world, dating back to 1598AD".

"Are you saying that the Freemasons are somehow mixed up in money laundering, the Mafia, murder and God knows what else?" I asked?

"Not at all." my father said. "The Freemasons are a long established, honorable organization, whose members have been, and still are, instrumental in many humanitarian endeavors. But like any organization as large as the Freemasons, subcultures often exist. One of these subcultures is believed to be the Illuminati. The illuminati did not originate from the Freemasons. It is believed that they infiltrated the Freemasons back in the 18th century, and have been recruiting members from the brotherhood ever since."

"So what are you saying?" I asked.

"It is Mino's and my opinion," said my dad, "that someone from inside the Freemason Lodge of Edinburgh, was enlisting carefully chosen men of prestige, power and money; people who have influence over others, into the Illuminati, and the men I was investigating were some of them!"

"Are you saying that you believe the Illuminati still exist, and were somehow involved with your client?" I asked.

"They had a profound involvement with my client, even though he was unaware of it at the time." my father said.

"The Illuminati, at its inception, was forced into existence, created, as it were, by the Catholic Church. Devoted, loyal men of the Church, were persecuted, tortured, and executed by the Church, for their studies of science and math, if their teachings conflicted with Church doctrines. Their properties were seized, their work discredited and they were subject to public humiliation. They were forced into exile and met secretively, sometimes literally underground, to continue their studies and exchange of ideas. This was the birth of the Illuminati. As the persecutions continued, and public executions increased, the Illuminati's numbers grew, as did distain for the Church. The Illuminati, who now consisted of some of the greatest minds of the time, vowed vengeance on the unjust, unholy acts of the Church. The two most powerful weapons at their disposal were intelligence and secrecy; something the Illuminati were exceptionally skilled at.

"It has long been suspected that throughout the years, the Illuminati infiltrated the Church at the highest levels, making it possible to influence Church doctrine in favor of a more scientific view of what is truth, over what is merely legend or tradition.

Over the years, the Illuminati extended its influence to include financial and political organizations. Some theorists now believe it is the intention of the illuminati to achieve global dominance. I don't know if that is true or not, but from the information I received from Mino, I *was* convinced in a connection between the Illuminati, the dig in Giza, my client and the murder of all those people that day.

"When I was questioned by the Egyptian authorities about my possible involvement or knowledge of the illegal activities in Giza, and the murders of my client and his associates, I was more determined than ever to continue my investigation, clear my name and protect my reputation.

"With Mino's help, I was introduced to some Freemasons, as someone interested in joining their brotherhood. It took several months, but little by little I met more of the members, and eventually, I was introduced to Father Heiss. Of course, I knew who he was before my introduction, but he did not know that. Although he was pleasant, there was something about him that made me feel uncomfortable. When he looked at me, it felt like he was invading my personal thoughts and contaminating me, if that makes any sense".

"I think I know what you mean." I said. "I have not had that much contact with him, but the few times I talked to him, I remember thinking that he was looking right through me, leaving nothing unknown to him about me. It was very unnerving. I don't know how Rune stands it."

My father continued. "As the months went by, I was able to make friends with a few of the members that I felt were a little less virtuous than the majority of the brotherhood. I was correct in my assessment of their character. After winning their trust, although I knew that trust was limited, I was able to extract information from some of them which confirmed Mino and my suspicions about the Illuminati's recruiting tactics. The head recruiter was none other than Father Heiss. He did not, however, attempt to recruit Mino or myself, despite our obvious willingness to join. That made me very nervous.

"One of the men I pretended to befriend had a real gift of gab. He liked to think of himself as more essential to the "big picture" than he was. This gave him the occasion to boast about things he should have kept to himself. I learned from him that a little over a year ago, certain members of the Illuminati within their ranks were responsible for the theft of billions of dollars from a bank in Italy. The money was used to fund a very secret project. He claimed to have firsthand knowledge, that it involved some kind of archeological dig in Egypt, and that the Vatican was directly involved. Other than a small amount of the stolen money being used for the dig, he did not know how the remainder of the money was used. He claimed, however, to have heard rumors, a large chunk of it was used to pay for some highly sophisticated, and experimental, lab equipment. I was convinced I would soon have enough information to be able to put all the pieces together and discover who hired my client, murdered him, and the reason behind it all".

I remember thinking to myself, "No wonder my father never mentioned any of this to me before. But why would any of this put Angela or myself in danger"?

Angela and I sat without saying a word, knowing my father would make the connection soon enough. I was not sure I wanted to know.

"It was shortly after speaking with my unwitting informant, when Mino contacted me and set up another meeting in Geneva." my father said. "It sounded urgent, and gave me cause for alarm. We met at the same coffee shop, and once again, sat outside.

"The moment I saw Mino, I noticed a look about him that was unsettling. His had a disheveled look about him, and looked like he hadn't slept in a week.

"Are you all right" I asked. "You look like hell"! He didn't answer my question, and went right into what he wanted to say.

"Mino leaned forward and reached across the small table and grabbed both my hands, which were resting on the table top, by the wrists. "You need to leave here immediately" he said. "Take a trip, go the States or something, but you need to leave now. Don't go home. If you need money I can help you"!

"Are you crazy" I asked. "What the hell is going on, Mino"?

"There is no time to explain everything now. Once you get out of here and are safe, I'll contact you, and explain everything" he said.

"I can't just up and leave" I said. "I have a son, or have you forgotten? What am I supposed to do, just leave him"?

"Your son! I'm sorry James, I forgot" he said.

"You forgot my son?" I asked. "What's wrong with you Mino? What happened to you"?

Mino took a deep breath and sat back in his chair, releasing my wrists, but never losing eye contact with me. He just stared at me for a few minutes, and it was unnerving. I looked at him, wondering if he had lost his mind. I knew Mino for many years. We worked together on several cases; some cases that put both of us in grave danger, but I'd never seen him like this.

"Last night," he said slowly, "I managed to sneak into a secret meeting with the Italian heads of the Illuminati. Don't ask how, I don't have time to explain. I discovered the location of the meeting, and was able to plant audio and video surveillance devices beforehand. I remained hidden throughout the meeting, but later realized my presence was known. I can't tell you everything I'd seen or heard, but what you need to know is that they know, James. They know everything! They know about me, and my investigation, about my working for the DIA. They know what I discovered about them, and they know about YOU! They know you contacted me to help investigate the murder of Dr. Osborne. They know what you learned about their involvement in the theft of money from that bank in Italy. They even had copies of the exact photos you sent to me when you first contacted me months ago. They even know about Mr. Shelton, that photographer you hired".

I could see that Mino was getting worked up again, and needed to calm him down. "Slow down Mino." I said. "Take it easy. Tell me what else you heard".

"I can't." he said. "It's too unbelievable. But if it's true, God help us all! They knew, James! They knew I was there and I heard everything! Yet they continued. They didn't care that I heard…heard what they…"

All the color drained from his face as his words fell into silence. That scared me more than anything else. What could he have heard that would scare him so bad he couldn't speak?

"Mino, are you all right?" I asked.

Mino leaned forward again and whispered. "You need to get out of here James. They are going to look for you. You and your photographer friend, and if they find you, they'll kill you." He reached into his jacket and took out a small tape. "Take this." he said. "Only when you are sure you're safe, listen to it. It will give you some idea of who you are dealing with. Hopefully it will convince you that I am right."

"What are you talking about?" I asked.

Mino got up from the table. "Go James, go now and never mention anything about your investigation, or anything you learned to anyone, ever. Maybe you still have a chance. Maybe."

"Mino!" I said. But he didn't answer me. He just got up and left, almost in a run. That was the last time I ever saw him.

"What happened to him?" I asked.

"He was murdered. He was found hanging under a bridge. They claimed it was suicide. I know he was murdered. That was in the winter of 1979." my father said.

Angela gasped! "Oh my God!" she said as she grasped my arm and hung on tightly.

"What was on the tape?" I asked.

"Most of it," my father said, "was a list of names, dates and events that reflected activity of the Illuminati. Some were criminal. Others, while not necessarily illegal, were definitely immoral. It also outlined the involvement of the illuminati in governing of religious, political and financial institutions." My father reached into the brief case and withdrew a folder and handed it to me. "This is a copy of a part of that tape." he said.

I took the file and Angela and I viewed the documents. The documents were basically a timeline of events, beginning in the early- fall of 1978, through mid-fall of 1979. It outlined the investigation into the alleged involvement of the Illuminati, in the murders of Pope John Paul I, Judge Emile Alexandrer, District Attorney Gorgio Ambroki, Detective Morris Gallano, and Lt. Col. Anthony Barico. Each of the victim was either witness to, or had an active role in the investigation of corruption within the Vatican and Banco Ambrosiano. One document also outlined the connection with the supposed perpetrators of those crimes, who were members of the Illuminate, with powerful government and business ties. One of the men under investigation was Bishop Paul Heiss of the Vatican Bank.

"My friend Mino was murdered in December of 1979 when he attempted to expose the illuminati and what he discovered about their master plan for humanity." my father said.

"This is incredible." I said. "How can they get away with this?' I asked.

"Money and power!!" my father said. "So much of both, that it is beyond the imagination. There was more on the tape. The tape spoke about a child. A baby boy. I don't know anything about the baby except the Illuminati put all its faith and resources behind him. This baby would hold the key to the future of everything the Illuminati hoped to achieve. Although I cannot prove it, I believe this baby was, and is, Rune Mikkell."

Chapter 10

The story my father was telling, gave me a sinking feeling deep in my chest. To this day, I don't know if it was anger, confusion or just plain fear. Could Rune possibly be tied up in such an evil group as the Illuminati? I have known him all my life, and there was nothing I ever witnessed that would suggest to me that he could have any involvement with such evil. I knew his adoptive parents. They were wonderful people. But then again, there is Cardinal Heiss, and Rune himself has doubts about the Cardinal and his tutors.

"After Mino's death, I met with Mr. Shelton." my father continued. "We discussed our options, and decided that our lives, and the lives of our family, were far more important to us than my reputation, and for the first time in my life, I made the decision to drop a case. We did not know if the Illuminati were after us, or even knew where we were, but we could not take that chance. We felt if we never spoke of any of this again, and kept under the radar, we might just get through this alive. Up until now, we were successful. However, with your investigation of Rune's origins, I am afraid that you may have put a spotlight on yourself and the rest of us."

"I'm so sorry dad," I said. "If I had known, I would never have accepted the job, not even for Rune."

"It's not your fault, son." said dad. "What we need to decide is where to go from here."

"I have a question." asked Angela. "Mr. Claiborne, when you met with Mino in Geneva, he asked you to take care of his daughter if anything should happen to him, and you promised you would. Whatever happened to her?"

My father fell back in his chair. I saw the color in his face drain, and knew this could not be good! Then, he turned and looked at Mr. Shelton and my heart felt like it was about to split open.

"Angela," said Mr. Shelton, "when your mother died in that auto accident so many years ago, she was not alone. My daughter was in that car as well. She too was killed that night. In one brief moment my entire world was taken from me."

I could see the tears swell in his eyes, and his words were choked in his throat. I turned to look at Angela, and as the realization of what he was saying overtook her, she began to tremble with overwhelming emotion.

"You needed me, sweetheart," Mr. Shelton cried, "and I needed you. Oh my God how I needed you! I fell in love with you the moment I saw you and held you in my arms. I swear to you, you could not be any more my daughter than if you were born of my own body, please believe me!" he cried.

Angela jumped from the sofa and ran out the door. I chased after her, and caught up to her in the driveway. I wrapped my arms around her and held her tight to my chest. I could feel her body heave with labored breath and sobs. Now I understood why my father wanted Mr. Shelton to be here. I didn't know if I should be angry with him, or thankful that all the secrets were now out. Angela had a right to know. I just didn't know if that was the best way to tell her.

"Do you want to go back in?" I asked her.

"I can't," she said, "not now."

"I understand." I told her. "You know he really does love you, and I am sure he is hurting as much as you right now."

"I know that," she said, "and I love him too! I could not have asked for a better father. But I need time." she cried.

"Why don't you get into the car, and I'll drive you home?" I said. "I'll let them know we need to leave. They'll understand." I helped her into the car, and went back into the house. Mr. Shelton was still crying, and my dad, looking very uncomfortable, was trying to console him.

"I'm going to take Angela home." I said. "I think we both need some time to process all this. Mr. Shelton," I said, "this has been quite a shock for Angela, but she loves you very much, you know that. She just needs some time, that's all."

"That you Robert." Mr. Shelton said. "I never wanted to hurt her. I love her so much. I told myself that I kept the truth from her to protect her, and in a way, that is the truth, but I know a part of me didn't want her to know, because I didn't want to share her with anyone. I wanted her to be my daughter, no one else's. I hope she can forgive me."

"She will, she does." I said. "I'll talk to her tonight. Dad, I'll see you tomorrow O.K? We have a lot to talk about."

"Good night son." dad said. "I'm sorry about all this. Somehow I feel it's all my fault."

"It's not your fault, dad." I said. If anything, you and Mr. Shelton should be proud. You kept Angela and me safe all these years from some of the most dangerous people in the world. We thank you for that. We'll talk tomorrow, Angela needs me now. Goodnight dad, goodnight Mr. Shelton."

It was a long ride home. I took Angela to my place. I didn't want her to spend the night alone. Neither of us slept well, and Angela stayed wrapped in my embrace the entire night. My heart was broken. I could feel her pain in my entire being. As I pressed my body tight to hers, I tried to envision absorbing her pain. A crazy, childish thing I know, but I would do anything to take it from her. She was my love, my life, everything I knew to be good in my world. I knew it would pass, but I also knew she would never be completely the same again.

Morning did not bring the usual light and joy I felt when I woke with Angela in my arms. I knew it would be a difficult day. I got up as quietly as I could, trying not to disturb my love. I made coffee, but not breakfast. I was not hungry, and didn't think Angela would be either. A short time later, she came from the bedroom. She looked better than I expected, although she lacked the cheer I was accustomed to when she entered a room.

"Good morning." I said. "How are you feeling?"

"Better than I probably look." she said.

"You look beautiful." I said.

"You don't look too well." she said. "I'm to blame for that I guess."

"I made coffee. I didn't make breakfast, because I wasn't sure if you would be hungry. Would you like me to make you something?" I asked.

"No, thank you." she said. "I couldn't eat right now. But I'll have some of that coffee."

We sat down and had a quiet cup of coffee, neither of us bringing up what happened the previous night. I remained silent, waiting for Angela to break the silence.

"I'm sorry I ran out on my father last night." she said. "I probably hurt him badly, and I didn't mean to do that. I just couldn't hear anymore. I'm so sorry. I know he never meant to hurt me, and I know he loves me."

"I'm sure he understands." I said. "It was a difficult thing for both of you to face."

"He *is* my father. I wouldn't want any other. I want him to know that."
Angela said.

"He needs to hear that." I said.

"Will you take me to see him?" she asked, "I don't want to go alone."

"You'll never be alone as long as I'm alive." I said.

She started to cry again and ran to my arms. I hugged her and kissed her.
"Get dressed." I said. "Maybe we can see him this morning."

The meeting with Mr. Shelton and Angela went well. Both cried, both
apologized, and both forgave each other. It made my heart feel warm to see
how they could overcome this and continue their relationship as father and
daughter.

The rest of the day, Angela, Mr. Shelton, my father and I discussed the
events that happened during the period of my father's investigation, the death
of Mr. Osborne and his team, as well as the death of Angela's birth father. We
compared information my father and Mr. Shelton had with the information I
had uncovered in my investigation. I brought up the death of Sister Mary Clarence, which now took on a whole new light. Did I, indeed, wake a sleeping
giant? Have I started a chain reaction of events that will spiral out of control,
putting everyone I love in danger? Was it too late to stop? I knew the decision
ultimately was mine, and I alone would be responsible for whatever might
come from it. After careful consideration, I decided that the best thing for me
to do was to take everything I knew to Rune, and together, we would make the
decision to continue, or back out.

Chapter II

I called Rune using the cell phone he gave me. He answered after only two rings.

"Hello Robert." Rune said. "How are you?"

"Could be better." I answered. "I think we need to meet. I have a lot to talk to you about that I cannot discuss over the phone."

"I see." he said "I have a very busy schedule right now. I don't know how closely you follow world events, but there is a crisis at the World Bank, and I have been asked to officiate a special meeting with the presidents of many of the world's largest banks. I need to be in Geneva tomorrow."

"This is very important, Rune." I said. "I wouldn't have called you otherwise."

There was silence on the other end for a few moments. Then I heard Rune.

"I see. Give me a minute." he said.

Rune put me on hold, and I had the sense that he may have been a little upset at my request. I didn't care. This was very important to me. I was doing this for him in the first place.

"Robert." Rune said. "I will see you tomorrow at my home around 10AM." It sounded more like a command than a request.

"I'll be there." I said. "What about the meeting in Geneva?" I asked.

"I postponed it for now." he said. "I'll see you tomorrow. I have a lot to do before then. Thanks for the call."

With that, he hung up. I was a little surprised at the tone of the conversation. Rune sounded a little disturbed by my call. But then he is a very busy man. That's when it struck me. An emergency meeting in Geneva had been arranged to be held in Geneva with many of the world's leading bankers. They were very important, very influential, and very busy people. Yet in less than two minutes, Rune postpones the meeting, and changes everyone's plans. In just two minutes! How could Rune have so much control? How powerful has he become?

No one met me at the airport this time. I took a taxicab to Rune's home, and called his phone on the way. Rune answered, and sounded much more pleased to hear from me than the day before. I told him I was in en route and should arrive in about twenty minutes.

When Rune answered the door, I immediately noticed how much older he seemed. I think all of his responsibilities were beginning to take its toll on him.

"It's so good to see you again." Rune said. "I'm sorry I didn't meet you at the airport, but I have been trying to get caught up on some of my work before you arrived."

"That's all right." I said. "It was a good flight, and I don't mind taking a taxicab."

"Nonetheless, it was rude of me, forgive me." he said. "Please come in and make yourself comfortable. Can I get you a cup of coffee, or something to eat?"

"No, I'm fine." I said. "Well, maybe a coffee. That's one habit I can't seem to break." Rune went into the kitchen, and I waited for him the parlor. I was a little nervous, not sure how he would take what I was about to reveal to him.

Rune returned with the coffee, and Danish muffins, and placed the tray on the coffee table. He sat down across from me, and as he settled in, he looked at me and asked "So, what do you have for me?"

I took out all the files and documents that my father gave me, and placed them on the table. As Rune reviewed the documents and files, I told him what I had discovered from my own investigation, and then covered the information revealed to me by my father. Throughout the entire revelation, Rune never spoke a word. He did, however, read over the files multiple times.

"That's everything I have for you right now." I told Rune as I concluded my story.

"This is all very alarming." Rune said. "But the thing I find most disturbing is the involvement of Cardinal Heiss, and the baby boy that your father suspects, is me. Nonetheless, the evidence, circumstantial as it is, does seem to suggest that he is correct. I must know the truth, Robert. This is very important to me. Even if Cardinal Heiss was the one who brought me to the orphanage, it still does not provide me with the information I am seeking – that is, who are my real parents?"

"Agreed," I said, "but there is more here than just the discovery of your birthright. If this information is true, and I have no reason to doubt my father, we are talking about some serious crimes, to include the murder of many innocent people."

"You are correct, of course." said Rune. "Any information that you may discover involving the perpetration of any crime, we will, of course, turn over to the appropriate authorities. We must, however, be very sure, before we accuse anyone. As you said, these are very serious crimes, and to accuse someone that may be innocent, would have profound consequences on their lives."

"I understand that," I said, "but don't you think we have an obligation to give what information we have to the authorities, and let them decide how to handle it?"

"I understand your concern, and I share it with you." Rune said. "But let's consider this. These crimes, if they in fact did occur, were committed many years ago. Also, your father was in possession of this information for quite some time, and, understandably, withheld it from the police. I know your father, and don't believe he would do that, even to protect himself or his family, if he was certain that the

crimes alleged in these documents happened, and he knew who the guilty parties were."

"Are you suggesting that we do nothing?" I asked.

"Not at all." Rune said. "If this information is correct, I want the guilty brought to justice as much as you do. I think, however, that we should proceed with caution."

"Then you do wish for me to continue with my investigation?" I asked.

"I understand the possible danger you and your family face. It is not my wish to put you or your loved ones at risk." Rune said. "But Robert, this is very important to me. Not just because of my professional standing, but because I need to know who I am! The information you have already uncovered is a great testimony to your abilities, and I am very thankful for what you have done. But I need you to continue. It is a lot to ask, I know. I will give you whatever help I can. I am not without influence, and may be able to provide you with some degree of protection. I do not guarantee your safety, or the safety of your family. But I will do all in power to protect you. Please Robert, I need your help."

That was the first time I have ever seen any hint of vulnerability in Rune. I really believed he needed me, and that I could help him. I considered the risk to myself, my family, and even to Rune, should things go wrong. After all was said and done, I decided to continue with my investigation. Partly because of my friendship for Rune, and a true desire to help him, if I could. But it was not because I felt I owed it to him, or because I didn't want to quit my first real investigation. It was

because I felt it was the right thing to do – for myself, for my father, for all those innocent people that lost their lives!

I gave Rune my decision to continue with the investigation, focusing first on the identity of his parents, as he requested. He was very pleased.

"Thank you Robert." he said. "I will not forget this. As I promised, I will help you anyway I can. To start, I opened a safety deposit box at the Zurich Cantonal Bank on Bahnhofstrasse. In that box, you will find some helpful items, to include enough cash in several currencies to cover any expenses. I felt that cash would help to conceal any paper trails of your transactions, should you wish to remain undetected."

"Were you that sure I would want to continue?" I asked.

"Not sure," Rune replied, "I was just hopeful! Now, do you know where you will begin?"

"I think the obvious place for me to start would be with the Church." I said. "If it is true that Cardinal Heiss was the one who brought you to the orphanage, which I think is a pretty sure bet, then there must be some record of how that occurred somewhere, and that record has to be with the Church."

"That is true." Rune said. "I may be able to help you there. During my tutelage, I developed a friendship with a priest by the name of Father Ethier, now Cardinal Ethier. We still remain in close contact today. Cardinal Ethier instructed me on the overall operations of the *Judicial Office* within the Vatican. He held a position in that office, second only to the General Secretary. Cardinal Ethier is a very good and honest man. If anyone can help you, he can. I will contact him, and tell him to expect you, if that is all right with you."

"The information I will be looking for is something someone wishes to keep secret. Can you trust this man?" I asked.

"As I said," said Rune, "he is an honest, and I believe trustworthy, man. If he can help us, I believe he will. All I can do is ask him."

"Excellent!" I said. "I will begin there. I should be able to leave for Vatican City in a couple of days. There are a few things I need to take care of at home first. Angela has been through a lot, and I need to be there for her right now."

"I understand." said Rune. "That brings up another issue. I think it might be best if you did not involve Angela in your investigation. If it is true that the Illuminati were responsible for the death of her father, her life may be in more danger than you know. Mr. Shelton was right to keep her true identity a secret. I don't think you should expose her now. At least until we know where this all leads."

I gave some serious thought to what Rune suggested, and I realized the wisdom of what he said. I agreed, and assured Rune that I would continue the investigation alone. I did not want to risk putting anyone else in danger if possible. Rune gave me the information I would need to access the safety deposit box he secured in my name, the personal telephone number of Cardinal Ethier, and a key to his home. "I want you to feel free to use my home whenever you need it." Rune said. "You may want to get away and regroup from time to time, and this will be as secure a place to stay as any I know. If there is anything else I can do to help, I want you to call me. After all, you *are* working for me, and you cannot do your job as expected, without my support."

I thanked Rune and assured him I would keep him informed as to how my investigation was going.

"I've cleared the rest of the day for you." Rune said, "so now that business has been taken care of, what do you say we take the rest of the day and enjoy ourselves."

"That sounds great." I said. "What do you have in mind?"

"How would you like a tour of the Vatican?" Rune asked.

"You have access to the Vatican?" I asked.

"You would be surprised at what I have access to." Rune said.

Chapter 12

The first thing I did when I got home was to call Angela and see how she was doing. She claimed to be doing fine, but I was not so sure. I made a date to pick her up for dinner, and arrived at her apartment a little after 6PM.

"God I missed you!" I told her. "You are all I could think about for the last couple of days. How are you?" I asked.

"I'm doing better than I thought I would." she replied. "Dad and I, that is, Mr. Shelton and I, spent the day together yesterday."

"I'm sorry Angela, but that sounds a little cold." I said.

"I didn't mean it to." she said. "It's just that I don't know how to explain my feelings. I now know that I had a different father. And Mr. Shelton, although he is the only dad I have ever known, is not my true father. I feel almost guilty, like I am denying my real father by calling someone *else* dad. Does that make any sense?" she asked. "After all, it's not like my father abandoned me or anything. He was murdered. And before he died, he did everything he could to protect me, and see that I was taken care of. How can I call someone else dad without dishonoring him?" she asked.

"You don't dishonor your father by calling Mr. Shelton dad." I said. "Mr. Shelton loves you like his own daughter, and I know you love him. I am sure that is exactly what your father wanted for you. I think it might be more of a dishonor to him by not accepting the love he made possible for you. Please don't let this news about who was your *real* father, destroy the relationship you have with the man you've known and loved all your life."

"You are right, of course." she said. "I *do* love Mr. Shelton, and I could not ask for a better father. I can't imagine life without him. Thank you Robert, you helped me to realize how important he is to me. What would I ever do without you?"

"You will never have to find out." I said. And with that, I gave her a big kiss and we held each other for a long time.

We went to our favorite restaurant for dinner, and shared a bottle of very expensive wine. That is not something we would normally do, but somehow, it seemed fitting. It felt like a celebration, in a strange sort of way. When we were enjoying the wine, Angela asked the question I was dreading.

"How did things go with Rune yesterday?" she asked.

I was worrying about how I would explain that I planned to continue the investigation into Rune's identity, and that I was going to proceed without her help. I decided to just come out with it, and hope for the best.

"I went over everything with Rune." I explained, "from what I discovered in my investigation, to the death of Sister Mary Clarence, as well as what my father and your dad shared with us."

"He must have been shocked," Angela said, "especially about the involvement of Cardinal Heiss."

"He was." I said. "I don't think he accepts everything my dad said as completely accurate, or at least not as fact without further proof."

"Didn't you show him the documents your father gave you?" she asked.

"Yes, and he studied them carefully." I answered. "I think it's difficult for him to believe that Cardinal Heiss could be mixed up in something so sinister. I believe he hopes I will find evidence that someone else was responsible and that Cardinal Heiss was an innocent participant in something he knew nothing about."

"Wait a minute," she said, "did you say he hopes you will find evidence? You are *not* going to continue working for him on this, *are you Robert?*"

"I gave it a lot of thought." I said. "I think I have to. I accepted the job, and I have a responsibility to see it through."

"You did not have all the facts when you agreed to work for him." she said. "You had no idea that a simple investigation would put you and your family in mortal danger!"

"I know." I said. "But I feel it's something I must do. I have information that may prove the guilt of men who were responsible for the death of several innocent people, not to mention about a dozen other crimes."

"Then give that information to the police. Let them handle it." Angela said. "It is not your responsibility."

"This is information my father held onto for decades." I said. "If what is in those documents turns out to be true, my father could be charged with obstruction of justice, and withholding evidence in a murder investigation – a murder investigation in which he was a person of interest. He could be sent to prison, when all he is guilty of is trying to protect his family. If the information he gave me is accurate, it is better that it comes from me. Besides," I said, "I feel that my investigation into Rune's past and these crimes are somehow connected. If I'm right, I may be getting involved with some pretty dangerous and powerful people. That is why I must do this on my own. I want my dad, your father, and most importantly you, as disconnected with the investigation as possible."

"You plan on doing this on your own, with no help from any of us?" Angela asked.

"I won't be completely alone." I said. "Rune will give me as much help as he can. He has connections that will be very helpful."

"That's not fair!" she cried. "You could be in serious danger. I could lose you. Please Robert, don't do this. Let the police handle it. Forget about Rune's parents. What difference does it make after all these years anyway? I need you! I love you! I couldn't live without you."

I pulled her close to me and held her in my arms. I kissed her lightly on her forehead. "Nothing will happen to me, you'll see." I said. "I am a very cautious man."

She buried her head in my chest and whispered "You don't know that Robert. I could lose you."

I didn't answer her. She was right!

Chapter 13

Rune met with the world's leading financial captains on June 13th, just two days after our last meeting. As crucial as the first summit was which Rune facilitated, it dwarfed in comparison to this latest threat to the world economy. War had broken out in Iraq for a second time in less than ten years. This time the country was under attack by radical and anarchistic ideologue terrorists, who seized control of the second largest oil field and refinery in the world. Other OPEC nations, afraid of a similar takeover, activated their military in the event of a showdown. Some Middle East nations with nuclear capabilities, like Israel and Pakistan, seemed ready and willing to deploy their weapons if their boarders were threatened. Super power nations like Russia and China were considering military options to prevent a nuclear exchange. The United States, weakened by decades of war, seemed reluctant, or unwilling to involve itself in yet another conflict. As a result of world events, every country faced imminent financial collapse. The U.S. dollar's role as the world's primary reserve currency, was rapidly coming to an end, in place of the Euro, which didn't fare much better in the world market. As a result, worldwide panic! Even countries that had no vested interest in the current military conflicts taking place in the Middle East, were in jeopardy of financial collapse, due to the symbiotic nature of the world economy.

In the meantime, I had my own agenda to focus on. I was going to meet with Cardinal Ethier in the morning, and I was not sure how much I should reveal to him, or exactly what his role would be in my obtaining confidential Church records. It was obvious that Rune trusted him, and since it was Rune who arranged the meeting, I felt I had a fair amount of latitude in that regard, but decided I would still use caution when I spoke with him.

I was nervous when I entered Vatican City. I didn't know if I felt that way because of piety, or subterfuge on my part!

I arrived at the *Palace of the Governorate* at 9:15A.M., and Cardinal Ethier, expecting my arrival, was there to meet me as soon as I entered the reception area. He quickly ushered me into his private office, giving me the feeling that he wanted me to have as limited interaction with his receptionist

as possible. Perhaps he was afraid I would divulge too much information regarding the reason for my visit.

"Please, have a seat." he said. "Rune speaks very highly of you, Robert.
He tells me you two have been good friends since childhood. I'm sorry we
have not met before."

"Thank you Cardinal, Rune speaks highly of you as well." I said. "It appears you were a profound influence in his life."

"I doubt that," he said, "but thank you for the compliment."

I found the Cardinal to be extremely personable, and easy to talk to. I was
not sure if that was a good thing or not. I explained to him that Rune contracted
me to investigate his history before his time at the orphanage. I told him that
my investigation led me to the Church, and more specifically, Cardinal Heiss.
I deliberately left out any information I had regarding the Illuminati and any
connection the Cardinal may or may not have had with them. I explained that
the records at the orphanage were lost, and the school Rune attended was unable to help. I asked Cardinal Ethier if he was aware of any records retained
by the Church that would help me.

Cardinal Ethier appeared pensive as he walked toward the window. After
a few moments of silence, he turned to face me. "I am in a very precarious situation. I have my loyalty to the Church, and the trust of this office to consider
on one hand, and my friendship with Rune on the other." he said.

"There is something else to consider." I said.

"Oh, what's that?" he asked.

"Doing the right thing." I said.

He turned from me and looked again at the window. "Yes," he said, "there
is that." Slowly he turned toward me. "How much do you know about Cardinal Heiss?" he asked.

Now it was *I* that was in a precarious situation. Should I tell him what I
know, or pretend ignorance? Would it be fair to ask him to betray his oath to
his office and the Church, while I withheld information, or even worse, lied
to him? It should have been an easy decision, but it wasn't, and that made me
question my own morality.

"Your silence speaks volumes, my friend." the Cardinal said. I felt betrayed by my own action, or lack of it! I realized I had a lot to learn as an
investigative journalist.

"Very well." he said. "What we speak of today will never be spoken of again, agreed?"

"Not even to Rune?" I asked.

"Not even to Rune." he replied.

"I don't know if I can keep that promise." I said.

"You are an honest and godly man, Robert." he said. "I will trust you to do the right thing."

"You're putting a lot of trust in someone you just met." I said.

"I am a very good judge of character." he said. "It comes with the job, I suppose." He walked toward me, and put a hand on my shoulder. "Before we begin, let us pray."

After prayer, Cardinal Ethier sat at his desk, and logged onto his computer. He printed out a very extensive file, and handed it to me.

"Thirty years ago," said the Cardinal, "I was an apprentice in this office. I was a young and ambitious lawyer, assigned to a case that involved the loss of several billion dollars from a bank outside Rome. The Vatican was involved; having provided letters of reference for several companies, which in turn allowed those companies to secure loans totaling hundreds of millions of Euro's each. It was later discovered that none of the companies involved actually existed, and they, along with all the money, disappeared without a trace. The person who authorized the letters of reference was a young priest assigned to the Vatican Bank. His name was Father Heiss. When questioned, Father Heiss insisted that his research of the companies involved, had demonstrated strong growth, sound economic strategies, and excellent credit histories. I asked him to provide the documentation used to make his determination, and he was unable to do so. He blamed the loss of records on a malfunction of the computer system, which contained all the files associated with the companies. Due to the magnitude of the crime and effect on the Italian economy, I was prepared to pursue the matter with all the resources available to me.

About two weeks into the investigation, I was called to a private meeting with Cardinal Jessuip, President of the *Pontifical Commission for Vatican City*, which is the Vatican City legislator. I met with the Cardinal in a private meeting. In that meeting, I was requested to close my investigation, and turn over all information I had to his second in command. Having sworn an oath of obedience, I had no option but to comply.

"If you turned over your files, where did these come from?" I asked.

"I have served the Church faithfully my entire life." Cardinal Ethier said. "Vanity prevents me from stating how many years that has been. For all of those years, I have faithfully kept my vows to God, the Church and my Office – with one exception. When I was requested to turn over my files, I had already made discoveries that I found very troubling, which, I am ashamed to say, involved members of the clergy. Crimes were being committed, and I felt an obligation to prevent any future acts of violence. I kept a copy my files, and continued, without the knowledge of my superiors, to investigate what I considered to be crimes against humanity. What you hold in your hands are the results of that investigation."

I looked down on the file Cardinal Ethier handed me, and then back to the Cardinal. "I don't understand." I said. "How is all this connected to Rune's birth parents?"

"Cardinal Heiss is Rune's father, and the proof is in that file." he said.

I took a deep breath. It surprised me how willingly I accepted that information. I should have been shocked. But I wasn't "And his mother?" I asked. "Do you know who his mother is?"

"The only name that I was ever able to connect with Rune and Cardinal Heiss," he said, "was 'Steptoe'. I am assuming that is a last name. My attempt to locate her failed."

"Perhaps I will have better luck." I said. "I can't thank you enough for your help." I stood up and shook the Cardinal's hand. "I hope I haven't caused you any trouble."

"I knew that someday, I would have to explain my actions and be accountable for my sins." he said. "I pray some good will come out of it."

Chapter 14

Unlike the first summit, Rune, despite his miraculous language skills, had difficulty. Every nation was placing fault for the failing economy on other nations, the biggest targets being Iran, Iraq, Israel, Great Britain, and leading the pack, the United States, with greed, self-serving interests, ambition, and religion, being the principle offenders.

Rune found himself frustrated at the lack of understanding and unwillingness of nations to accept concessions in order to resolve this crucial situation. Rune questioned whether they understood the magnitude of what would happen in the event of a global financial collapse! A strong hand was needed, and Rune felt the time was now! If a proposal was made that could resolve all these financial issues permanently, and that proposal was presented decorously, Rune felt that most nations would be willing to accept it. They were, after all, just like sheep, looking for a shepherd.

Nonetheless, the reason for Rune's presence at the summit was for his abilities as an interpreter and Ambassador to Vatican City. It was not his place to make suggestions, especially one of such magnitude, no matter how strongly he felt the need.

Having dealt so deeply in world economy most of his professional life, Rune had given a great deal of thought on possible scenarios that might eliminate the threat of a worldwide financial collapse. He had, in fact, devised just such a financial plan, using a single global currency. This was not a new idea. Many world economists had made the suggestion before. The difference was, Rune had found a way to make it work! There have been strong opposition to the idea of a global currency by some of the world's leading financial geniuses, and their

concerns were justified. It would be a hard sell, but if anyone had the ability to make them understand the benefits of such a system, it was Rune.

"Distinguished Ladies and Gentlemen. May I have your undivided attention, please?" asked Rune. Almost immediately, the entire assembly fell silent. "I speak for myself now, not for any individual of this assembly, or representative of any nation or institution. It has been my pleasure to serve this dignified assembly as your interpreter and Ambassador for a second session on this most delicate and pressing matter. I would like to address this assembly, not in my capacity as either, but that of a witness to the event which is unfolding here. I see before me, the most acclaimed, honorable and knowledgeable men and women in the world of finance in the world. I have witnessed the struggle each of you endure, in an attempt to prevent the cataclysmic failure of our world's economy, without jeopardizing the trust and responsibility you have to your constituents. Your efforts have truly been commendable. In servitude to this committee, I have been in a unique position to know the heart and soul of each one of you, through your words. Words, in my opinion, are the most powerful weapon we humans possess. They have the ability to destroy, as well as the power to create. I know your words, and thereby know your intent, and they are honorable. And yet, here we are at an impasse."

Each member of the assembly gave quiet reflection on the fact that Rune could, in fact, know their minds and intentions, and that gave them some, disquieting concern!

"The world is depending on each and every one of you for their financial survival. Time is running out, and you are failing them." A loud rustle of voices spread throughout the assembly. Rune continued speaking above the din. "This is not your fault." Rune exclaimed in a thunderous voice. "I fear the problems you face today may be without resolution." The assembly fell silent once again."Ladies and gentlemen," Rune said, "it is not my intension to cause panic, nor is it in my nature to be an alarmist. However, we must acknowledge and face the truth once revealed. The primary difficulty that faces all of us is the ability for each nation to preserve the sovereignty of their currency, while living in a world dependent on the financial stability of others. This has not, and cannot, work!" Rune gave them a moment to digest his words.

"What do you suggest?" someone yelled out.

"The solution is an obvious once again the assembly was abuzz with discussion." Rune said. "We must convert to a single, global currency." Once again the assembly was abuzz with discussion.

"That proposal has been presented before," cried out a representative from China, "as recently as this year, and the opposition from many of our learned colleagues was staggering."

"Most of you know of my reputation, not only as an interpreter, but as a respected financier. I have devised a financial plan based on a single global currency that I believe would benefit every citizen of this planet. I can make a copy of my system available to each of you, for your review, if you so desire. The benefits of a single world currency," said Rune, "is undeniable. I do not wish to insult this distinguished assembly by stating the obvious, but the success or failure of such a system would be dependent, however, on one fact and one fact alone. It is not a question of whether the desired results are achievable, but rather, a question of trust. The success of such a system is undeniable, if, and only if, this assembly, as a whole, could agree upon election of a leader, trusted by all, who would have ultimate governing control of that system. This, I propose, should be the only issue of debate. No other solution is possible. The success or failure of this assembly, to prevent a cataclysmic collapse of our global economy, rests within your hands; not your ability to solve the individual financial problems of every nation, but to put your trust in one man; to bring an end to this otherwise endless conflict."

"Who would you suggest for such a task?" asked the representative of Great Britain.

"It is enough that you suffered my interposition, speaking outside my assigned duties of this summit." said Rune. "It is not my place to suggest who would qualify for such an onus charge. I must leave that lofty task to the judgment of this exceptionally qualified and honorable assembly."

The President of the World Bank stood and addressed the committee. "I request a recess in order for the members of this committee to consider Dr. Mikkel's words, and request a copy of the plans for a one world currency offered by Dr. Mikkel, for each member for review." Rune promised that a copy would be made available for each member of the assembly, first thing in the morning. The motion for recess was unanimous.

It was three days before the summit reconvened. Rune was present to assume his dual role as interpreter and Ambassador.

Once again, the President of the World Bank took the floor. A hush fell across the entire assembly. "For the past several days, my colleagues and I have had the pleasure of reviewing the files provided to us by Dr. Mikkel, outlining a most remarkable plan for incorporating a single world currency, and the feasibility of such a system. With little contention, this committee has overwhelming agreed that his system, in totality, be adopted by this committee, to be presented to our respective nations and approving authorities for consideration." The entire assembly stood and applauded the announcement. "There is one contingency, however. It was, by unanimous agreement, decided that success of this program would only be possible if it's officiate be Dr. Rune Mikkel. Therefore, upon acceptance from our respective governments, it is the honor of this committee to offer the position as President of the New World Order of Finance to Dr. Rune Mikkel. If accepted, Dr. Mikkel would have complete autonomy in regard to the implementation of his financial system, along with the authority to elect those of his choosing to assist him in the operations of the office. Will you accept such a charge Dr. Mikkel?"

Rune accepted the offer.

Chapter 15

Several months passed since Rune's nomination for the post of President of the New World Order of Finance. Without exception, every nation agreed to accept Rune's proposal of a single world currency, and his nomination. Rune was sworn into office one month after the final vote. Of course he was required to resign from his position at the Vatican Bank, and although it was with great regret, his resignation was accepted. Rune's financial system of a "one world currency" was a great success from its inception. There were a few holdouts, however. The United States, Great Britain, Australia, and Japan were reluctant to give up the dollar, the pound and the yen respectively. This was despite their acceptance of the newly created monetary system, which was based on a credit system, and eliminate hard currency altogether. Under the new order, credits earned would be used for purchases anywhere in the world, which would eliminate the inequality of those nations, whose economy was weakened due to the perception that one currency was stronger and held greater value than another. Rune quickly gained the respect and gratitude of the business world and civilians alike. Rune literally had his hand around the heart of the entire world economy. He was quickly becoming one of the most powerful and beloved men in the world.

Italy, France, Germany, China and Russia were some of the first countries to convert over to Rune's new financial system. Under Rune's guidance, everything was working well. An employee would be compensated for work done with the credits of a predetermined amount. This amount was paid regardless who or where the work was performed. Now, someone who performed a service in India was credited equally as someone who performed the same service in the United States, China or Japan. The credits were documented in the computer mainframe, under the control of his or her employer. Credits could be bought, sold and loaned, just as in the case of hard currency. On a weekly basis, the employee would receive a statement indicating the amount of credits earned that week. Each employee received a card, much like the debit card we have all come to know, and it alone, would be used for purchases at any establishment in the participating nations. It worked very much like money, only no hard currency was ever exchanged, and the credits were accepted anywhere in the world. A debit of credits were verified against the total credits maintained in the computer mainframe of the local banking institutes. It seemed like a perfect system; and it was, for a short time! It did not take long before someone discovered a way to counterfeit the debit cards. Shortly after, credits, like money before it, was being stolen, misappropriated, or embezzled. Disreputable banks and businesses were able to falsify credit deposits, or work performed. Goods were not being paid for, or over paid; workers were not credited with what they earned, and in a short time, what should have been a perfect financial system, was under the threat of collapse.

Rune called an emergency meeting of world leaders, to address the imminent danger.

"It is with deep regret," Rune addressed the assembly, "that I call you here today. Each of you has acknowledged the merits of the New World Order Financial System you have chosen, in hopes of rectifying the global financial instability we have lived with for far too long. You have given me charge of that system, and I stand by my commitment to integrate that system throughout the world, knowing that it is the one and only hope we have to create a truly equitable financial program. Unfortunately, there remains an element of corruption that is determined to undermine this revolutionary approach. This undesirable element of human behavior focuses on self-interest and ill-gained profit, at the expense of others. I have spent a great deal of time contemplating how we can prevent this corruption from destroying all we have worked so hard to accomplish. There is but one solution to our problem. We must take away the teeth and claws of this enemy! I am referring to the debit card and mainframe computers that are the heart of our system."

Whispers could be heard throughout the assembly.

"How is that possible?" asked the representative of the U.K. "The system you have put in place relies on the ability for each citizen to purchase goods and services solely with the use of these cards. With the elimination of hard currency, our computer systems are the only possible way to maintain accountability of each personal or business account."

"And yet," replied Rune, "it is these same, trusted systems, that are being abused, infiltrated and manipulated, by the corrupt elements mentioned, determined to undermine our success. It is for that reason, I suggest the use of a single, super computer, headquartered at the World Bank, controlled through a single entity.

Hold one person responsible for all." Rune responded. "Eliminate third party access, and you eliminate corruption. You have pulled the teeth of the tiger."

"How would our citizens access their credits without cards or currency?" asked the representative of New Zealand.

"By bar code." answered Rune. "Each individual would receive a bar code, as individualized as a finger print, which would only be visible by infrared scanners, placed on the hand. Without this bar code, and thusly without the person, no credits could be exchanged. Theft would be impossible. With the implementation of a single controlling super computer, misappropriation of credits would become impossible. Embezzlement of funds would become a crime of the past. For those unfortunates that have loss of limb through accident or birth defect, the bar code would be placed on the forehead."

"What you are proposing sounds very much like the 'Sign of the Beast' as described in Revelations of the Christian Bible." said the representative of the United States. "The resistance to the use of such a mark would be overwhelming."

"There is, I agree," said Rune, "an alarming resemblance. But we must face facts. There is no cynical element in play here, only a logical, practical way to put an end to financial corruption once and for all. I am sure that most people will be able to understand that. For those that argue otherwise, I would challenge them to make the connection of the 'Mark of the Beast', which scripture clearly identifies to be three sixes, and the placement of a bar code for commerce. If a legitimate connection can be made, I will withdraw the suggestion. I am as well versed in the scriptures as anyone, having studied them my entire life. I can assure you all, if I could make a rational connection between the two, I would be the first to proclaim it. I have earned the trust of the multitudes; I have always done what is best for all mankind, regardless of race, religion or national origin, and would never do anything to endanger anyone. The actions of my entire life are testament to my commitment to the truth."

"It is true, you are known throughout the world as a man of peace, and have earned the trust of many people." said the representative of the U.K. "Still, is it enough? You are calling into question a belief held by many in my country alone. Christians throughout the world will protest and many will refuse to receive such a 'mark' regardless of your assurances. If even a few refuse, the project will fail."

"I have faith in the people to come to the correct decision." said Rune. "All I ask is a chance to let the people decide."

After a few minutes of mumbling throughout the assembly, the representative of Russia spoke. "Ladies and Gentlemen. I believe we all will need time to consider what Dr. Mikkel has proposed today. I motion that we recess for one week, in order to present to our colleagues and leaders of our respective nations, the proposal brought before us today. If Dr. Mikkel would be able to meet us here, say in ten days, I feel we would be better equipped to make a decision regarding his proposal. All in favor?" The assembly agreed, and was dismissed.

Rune was pleased!

Chapter 16

I was still deeply involved with the investigation into Rune's past, although I was not certain that it held the same urgency to Rune that it once did. Nonetheless, I was determined to get some answers, not only for Rune's sake, but for myself, and my family. I found the information shared by Cardinal Ethier to be very helpful. It took me a little time, but eventually, I began to see a pattern emerge. It should have come to me sooner. One of the time-honored traditions of investigative reporting is "follow the money"!

I began with the assumption that Cardinal Ethier and the documents he gave me were correct, and Cardinal Heiss was Rune's father. I began there. What I learned with the help of Cardinal Ethier about Cardinal Heiss, which I was unaware of, was that he appeared to be involved with the disappearance of billions of dollars, which took place several years before the birth of Rune. I also knew that he was in Egypt shortly after the theft, and on more than one occasion, had contact with Michele Sindona (Alias Charles Schmitt). Mr. Sindona hired my father's client, James Claiborne, to perform an illegal dig in Egypt, financed by someone unknown, at enormous cost. Since the money was handled through a Swiss Bank, it was more difficult to trace, but not impossible - the how's and why's of getting that information is better left unsaid. Suffice it to say, that although I could not discover the name of the person on the Swiss numbered account, I was able to learn, with the help of Cardinal Ethier's documents, that the account originated through money that was transferred from the Vatican Bank. Cardinal Heiss worked for the Vatican Bank. Shortly after the incident in Egypt, in which all those involved with the dig were murdered, another significant amount of money was transferred, via the same Swiss bank account, to Steptoe Micro-Bioengineering Laboratory, in the United States.

I contacted a friend from my college years, and incorporated his help with my research. Roger was a computer genius, and a pioneer in A.I. (artificial intelligence). He was able to devise a program that could cross reference names, dates, times, and places with events and provide hypothetical correlations. I gave him everything I had from my own investigation, my father's files, newspaper clippings and the file given me by Cardinal Ethier. I offered hypothetical scenarios, involving the archeological dig in Egypt, the illuminati, the Catholic Church, Italian Mafia, and all the people whose name appeared in my investigation. Since I was told by Roger that it may take several days before I get any results, I decided to track down Cardinal Heiss. I was curious as to what he would say if I presented Rune's birth certificate with his name listed as the father. It was a risky proposition, but one that I felt needed to be done. As it turned out, Cardinal Heiss left over 8 months earlier on a sabbatical, and would be gone for an undetermined amount of time.

I decided it was time to take a step back and plan my strategy, and where better than at home? Angela, her father, and my dad were glad to see me. They were worried that I might have found myself in difficulties that I would be unable to handle. I shared with them what I discovered, and what I hoped to discover with Roger's help. They were impressed with the progress I'd made, and my father expressed pride in my abilities, and what I had learned regarding my profession. We discussed the new monetary system, and debated the pros and cons as we saw it. But there was one thing that we all agreed upon. We were concerned about all the influence and power Rune seemed to be assimilating. What he had achieved in just a few years was nothing short of miraculous. Where have I heard *that* before?

Considering what Rune was now involved with, I was not sure how important my mission was for him anymore. I might even have considered giving the whole thing up, except now it had become personal. My family and the girl I loved was now involved. I am not sure how, but I do know that my father and Angela's adoptive father lived in fear for years. Angela lost her father, and my father lost a friend, and was a suspect in the murder of several men, including one of his clients. I may be in possession of information that would bring the murderer of those people to justice, and allow my father and Angela's to live the rest of their lives without fear. I truly believed that somehow, all this was connected to the discovery of Rune's past. I was *not* going to give up!

About three days after arriving home, I received a phone call from Roger at the University. He had the results I was waiting for, and he was sending the file to me via e-mail.

When the files arrived, I opened them immediately. The results were not far from what I had expected; still, it was enough to warrant a meeting with Rune. I called him immediately, using the secured phone and number he gave me. When he answered, I told him that I had information that he needed to be made aware of, and the sooner, the better. He explained his situation with the crisis he was in, regarding the *New Financial Order* and that as important as this information was to him, it would have to wait until after the next assembly. I agreed, and we made a date to meet at his home in a couple of weeks. I was glad, in a way, for the extra time. It would give me time to figure out how to explain everything, and what I think it all means. And there was another reason I could use the time as well. The computer program offered a suggested connection to the name "Steptoe", identified on Rune's birth certificate as his Mother. I would need time to investigate the possibility, although I could not see what connection there could be with the name of a biochemical laboratory in the U.S., and Rune's birth mother. One other thing that the report revealed; Cardinal Heiss was *not* Rune Mikkel's father!

Chapter 17

It was all over the news; covered by every news station, newspaper and reporter worldwide!

"Due to circumstances beyond the control of the New World Order of Finance, corruption, orchestrated by disloyal citizens working within the system, has necessitated implementation of a new mandate. This new mandate has been approved by the nation's leaders throughout the world. It has become necessary for each citizen of every nation, be it man, woman or child, to report to their local civil government headquarters no later than Friday, October 30th of this year. Each citizen, regardless of age, will be surrendering his or her debit card in exchange for the issuance of a personalized bar code. This new bar code will be used for future purchasing of all commodities. Without this code, purchases will be impossible."

I couldn't believe what I was hearing! This sounded like something right out of the scriptures. I could not believe that people would accept this mandate. Surely there would be protests from every Christian Church throughout the world. How could they possibly have gotten this passed by every nation! It would have taken a miracle! This had to be the work of Rune. He was, after all, the president of the New World Order of Finance. I needed to speak to him, and quickly. Once again, I called him to ask for a meeting.

"Hello Robert." Rune said, answering immediately, "I was expecting your call."

"Rune," I said, "what is going on? I just heard the news about this new mandate requiring everyone to get a bar code by the end of October."

"Isn't it great?" he replied. "I would never have gotten this passed, except for the help of Cardinal Heiss."

"I don't understand." I said. "What does Cardinal Heiss have to do with the New World Order of Finance?"

"It was actually his idea." Rune replied. "He presented the idea to me just before the last emergency assembly. It was an idea he had been working on for a long time. At first I was unsure of the feasibility of the program. I, like many other Christians, initially saw too great a semblance with the 'Mark of the Beast' mentioned in the Bible. However, with the help of the Cardinal, I was able to summarily dismiss the similarities. But enough about my success." he said. "I suppose you called to set a date for our meeting. I can see you this Monday, next. Will you be able to be there?"

"I will be there." I said. "You can bet on it."

The next day I was on a plane for Boston, MA. The laboratory that I wanted to visit was located in Cambridge, just outside Boston. It was called the "*Steptoe Bioengineering Laboratory*". I called ahead and made an appointment to speak with Professor Lindsley, assistant program manager assigned to international accounts. I arrived at the lab at 10:30A.M., and was greeted by a lovely redheaded receptionist. She asked me to have a seat, as she announced my arrival to Professor Lindsley.

Professor Lindsley turned out to be what I would call a typical looking biochemist, dressed in a white lab coat, with dress shirt and tie, and wore large black framed glasses. I received a cordial welcome, and was escorted to his office.

"Please have a seat Mr. Claiborne." he said.

"Please, call me Robert." I said.

"Robert. What brings you all the way to our small lab from Geneva?"

"Italy, actually." I corrected.

"What can we do for you, Robert?"

"I'm not sure about that myself." I answered. "I am working on a case for Dr. Rune Mikkel. You may have heard of him." I said.

"Indeed I have." said Professor Lindsley. "Anything I can do to help Dr. Mikkel, would be my honor."

"I am sure he would appreciate that. I am here because of a name that appeared on one of Dr. Mikkel's personal documents. A name that, up until only a few weeks ago, was unknown to him. That name is 'Steptoe'." I said.

"The name of our lab." he responded. "Surely there are many businesses and people with the name Steptoe." he said.

"Yes," I said, "but sources which I am not permitted to reveal, have linked the name directly to this lab. Is there any connection between this laboratory and Dr. Mikkel that you are aware of?" I asked.

"None that I know of." Professor Lindsley said. "But let me run Dr. Mikkel's name through our computer data base, and see if anything comes up. Could you provide me with an address for Dr. Mikkel?" he asked.

"I'm afraid that is confidential." I said. "I could tell you, however, that Dr. Mikkel resides in Lazio, Italy."

Professor Lindsley sat behind his desk and started typing information into his computer. He was the fastest typist I had ever seen! After a short time, he looked up from his computer. "I don't see any reference to Dr. Mikkel in our data base." he said. "As a matter of fact, I found only one account from Italy, and that was quite a few years ago."

"Is there a name associated with that account?" I asked.

"Yes, there is." he said. "The name is Paul Heiss."

My heart started pounding in my chest. What the hell is going on here I thought? "What information can you give me about that account?" I asked.

"It's quite old," he said, "I'm not sure if I have much detail available. From what I can tell, Paul Heiss was an investor of some kind." Professor Lindsley lifted both eyebrows, as if in amazement! "It appears that his *extremely* generous donation to our founder, Philip Steptoe, made this facility a reality. It is unclear what, if any, further connection existed between them. I have no other records suggesting any contact with Paul Heiss, Philip Steptoe, or this lab."

"Thank you, Professor." I said. "You have been very helpful. Oh, by the way, what does this lab specialize in, if I may ask?"

"At the moment," he said, "we are working on various projects, all related to bioengineering of living tissue and artificial materials, that are suitable for human implant. But when first established, Dr. Steptoe was working on cutting edge technology dealing with cloning."

"Thank you again professor, I will be sure and let Dr. Mikkel know of your cooperation. I have taken up enough of your valuable time. I will see myself out."

The next week flew by. There was news on every television and radio station about the new "stamp act", which is what everyone was now calling the bar code program. With each announcement, Runes picture was thrown in somewhere, giving him credit for putting an end to private and government corruption, once and for all. The theory was, since *"money was the root of all evil"*, and Rune put an end to money, then we were at a turning point in history, and much closer to world peace. It was even decided, in honor of this "peacemaker", a small photo of Rune, would be embedded within the bar code. There was even a contest in which anyone could vote on which photo to use on the chip. Choices were selected from the photos of Rune that were telecast on the daily news about the "stamp act". Of course there were some still in strong opposition. Mostly Christian groups, claiming it was the "*Mark of the Beast,*" and a few other pockets of protesters who simply did not want anyone to have that much control over their lives. Personally, I was one of the latter. I was very anxious for my meeting with Rune. Not only to reveal what my investigation had uncovered, but to express my feelings about his program, and the control he seemed to be taking over everyone's lives.

Before I knew it, Monday arrived, and I found myself outside Rune's door. I must say that I was pretty nervous, but I had all my evidence with me, and rehearsed in my mind many times, what I was going to say. I was a little un-comfortable when I noticed all the men, which I assumed were bodyguards that were watching his house. I wondered if I would be searched, and forced to turn over the berretta I had concealed under my jacket. They were obviously aware of my pending arrival, since they did not approach me, although they never took their eyes off of me.

They compared me to a photo they were holding, and seemed satisfied that I posed no threat. I rang the bell, and waited. When Rune opened the door, he seemed genuinely happy to see me.

"Robert," he said with a smile, "it's good to see you."

"You too." I said as we gave each other a brief hug. "Wow, you have as many bodyguards as the Prime Minister! What's that all about?"

"Well, unfortunately, in my business, not everyone who visits is a friend." he said. "Come in, come in and sit down. Can I get you something?" he asked.

"No," I answered, "I'm fine. I brought some documents with me for you to look over before I explain what I believe they mean."

"Robert," Rune said, "we haven't seen each other for a long time. Let's forget about business for a moment, and tell me, how have you been? How are your dad and Angela? It has been so long since I've heard from anyone. That's my fault, I know, but this business with the bar coding, I hate calling it a 'stamp act', has taken all my time."

"Yes," I said, "I can see how that could happen."

"Is something wrong, Robert?" he asked. "I mean that sounded a little cold."

"I'm sorry." I said. "It's just that this investigation proved to be more than I expected. And now, with this stamp act, sorry, I mean bar code program, well, I am finding it a bit mind-boggling."

"I see." said Rune. "Well, maybe we should get right to it then; save the small talk for later."

"It might be best." I said.

Rune led me into the living room, and we sat down with the coffee table between us. I placed my briefcase on the table, and took out my files.

"I know that you are up-to-date with my investigation, prior to my visit with Cardinal Ethier." I said.

"How is the Cardinal?" asked Rune.

"He is doing well," I said, "and he gave his regards. He was very helpful, and supplied me with a copy of a private file he retained for many years on Cardinal Heiss."

"It has become obvious that Cardinal Heiss has been a main factor in your investigation, and I wonder why?" Rune asked.

"It did not begin that way," I said, "but each turn I made investigating your early years, led me to him. It was Cardinal Heiss, then Father Heiss, who brought you to the orphanage, according the late Sister Mary Clarence. It was Cardinal Heiss that encouraged Mr. and Mrs. Mikkel to adopt you, and it was Cardinal Heiss that oversaw your education and training with the Church."

"That is enlightening," Rune said, "but does not provide an answer to the question you were hired to discover, that is, who are my parents!"

"Here is something you may be interested in." I said, and handed over a copy of Rune's birth certificate.

I watched Rune's expression as he read the document and the surprise on his face as he read the name, *Paul Heiss,* listed as his father.

"Cardinal Heiss is my father?" Rune exclaimed!

"That birth certificate was granted to Cardinal Heiss as a young priest per special dispensation." I explained. "However, I have reason to believe that the document was falsified."

"That's a very serious accusation." said Rune. "What is your evidence?"

"A copy of Cardinal Heiss's medical records shows, that as a child, he suffered from a condition called orchitis, which was a complication of having mumps. Later tests prove beyond a doubt, that the condition left Cardinal Heiss sterile. It would have been impossible for him to have fathered a child."

"I see." said Rune. I could tell that he was getting very upset. I don't know if it was targeted at me, or Cardinal Heiss. "And my mother." he said.

"What do you know about her? Have you found out anything about this Ms. Steptoe?"

"Very little." I said. "I tried to find any connection to the name Steptoe and Cardinal Heiss, since the birth certificate would suggest they knew each other intimately. The only connection I was able to make, however, was to a laboratory in the United States named *Steptoe Micro-Bioengineering Laboratory*. It seems that Cardinal Heiss was instrumental in funding the creation of the laboratory. What other significance it has, I do not know."

"I see." said Rune. I could see the anger in his eyes. "Is there anything else?" he asked.

"Not about your birth record." I said.

"But there is something you want to say." said Rune.

"Rune, you and I have been friends since childhood." I said. "It was because of that friendship that I agreed to do this investigation for you. But I have to tell you, I don't like where it's going. I know that you and your family have a long history with Cardinal Heiss, and that you have always respected and admired him for his service to the Church and your family. I also know that you consider him a close friend. But have you ever reflected on the complete picture? I mean, it is obvious that Cardinal Heiss has been involved, even *instrumental*, in every major aspect of your life; from your birth to your present position as president of the *New World Order of Finance*. It's as if he has been orchestrating events in your life to sculpt you into someone of his making."

"That is very unflattering to me personally, and challenging to Cardinal Heiss." said Rune. I could tell that he was trying to control his temper.

"I apologize." I said. "I don't mean to be; at least not to you, Rune. But the information I have discovered in regard to Cardinal Heiss, does not portray a very good person. I am sorry, but that is what I see."

"I respect your candor, Robert." Rune said. "However, I cannot say I agree with you. At the same time, I do not like being a puppet for anyone. If what you say is true, even to a limited extent, I cannot let it continue. I believe it is time that we have a meeting with Cardinal Heiss in person, and present him with what you have discovered. There is one point you make that I am certain of, and that is Cardinal Heiss is the only person who has the answers regarding my birth, and my birth parents. I don't know why he has chosen to keep this information from me, but the time for keeping secrets are at an end, and the time of revelation, begins."

Rune stood, walked over to his desk, and dialed a number on the phone. A few moments later, he was speaking to Cardinal Heiss.

"It is imperative that I see you as soon as possible." Rune said. "I will be bringing a friend of mine with me. You may remember him. His name is Robert Claiborne. Yes, that is him." Rune said to Cardinal Heiss. "This involves both of us. I believe his presence is necessary. Very well, we will be there at one o'clock this afternoon." Rune hung up the phone.

"You heard?" he asked.

"I did." I said. "Do you intend to show him everything I discovered?" I asked.

"I think it is the only right thing to do. Besides the issue of my birth, there are many other accusations made against the Cardinal, and I believe he should have to chance to answer them. Does this trouble you?" Rune asked.

"No." I said. "I would like the answers as well. If my assumptions are false, I will be the first to apologize, and will do everything in my power to see that the truth be known."

"That is very magnanimous of you." Rune said. "This is one time I hope you are wrong."

"Believe me," I said, "so do I!"

Chapter 18

We arrived at Cardinal Heiss's home just before 1:00P.M. It was a large, beautiful stone structure, and judging by the architecture, was hundreds of years old, and the landscape was exquisite. It did not fit the lifestyle of a Cardinal, but more of a nobleman. A gentleman answered the door, and I assumed he was a butler, or some other domestic servant. "Mr. Mikkel and Mr. Claiborne." he said. "You are expected. Please follow me." He led us to a room that looked like a library. "Please make yourselves comfortable." he said. "Cardinal Heiss will be with you shortly. Is there anything I can get for you in the meantime?" he asked.

"No thank you." Rune answered.

"Very well." he said. "If you change your mind, just pick up the phone and dial one." He left the room, closing the door behind him.

"Wow." I said. "I thought priests took a vow of poverty?" I asked.

"*Priests* would be the definitive word." Rune said. "It seems that no longer applies when one reaches a certain level of hierarchy in the Church."

It was just a few moments when the library door opened, and Cardinal Heiss walked in.

"Rune." he called out, with arms outstretched, seeking a recipient. "It is so good to see you again!" He gave a Rune a hug, and then turned to me. "And this must be Robert." he said with a smile. "I've heard a great deal about you, young man. It is a pleasure to finally meet you." He walked over to shake my hand.

"Thank you Cardinal." I replied and returned his handshake.

"Now, what seems to be the trouble?" the Cardinal asked, turning his attention back to Rune. "You mentioned that it was an urgent matter. Is everything all right?"

"No, Cardinal Heiss, it is not." Rune responded. "Robert is an investigative journalist that I hired some time ago, to investigate my early childhood; specifically, my birth, and the identity of my birth parents. In that endeavor, Robert has uncovered some very disturbing information, and much of it focuses you, Cardinal Heiss. Among other things, documentation that Robert has obtained, would suggest that you have direct knowledge about my birth. That documentation would also appear to verify that you have taken extraordinary steps, to include falsifying a legal document, to keep that information from being discovered."

"Those are very serious accusations." said Cardinal Heiss, with a smile. "May I see those documents?"

"Of course." said Rune, who handed the Cardinal a copy of the birth certificate. "There are other documents as well." said Rune, "that implicate you in the involvement of several crimes, some of them most serious."

"I see." said the Cardinal, as he examined the birth certificate given to him by Rune.

"Is that my birth certificate, and is that your signature on it, listing you as my father?" Rune asked.

"It is the certificate of your birth," Cardinal Heiss replied, "and yes, that is my signature."

"Can you explain that to me?" asked Rune. I was impressed at the maturity and decorum that Rune demonstrated. He did not appear to be the least intimidated by the Cardinal, and conducted himself in a manner suggestive of the Cardinal's equal.

"Is it not obvious?" the Cardinal asked. "I am your father, therefore my signature is on the document."

"Then can you explain this?" Rune asked, as he handed the Cardinal another document. "This is a copy of your medical records. They verify that as a child, you contracted a common childhood disease; mumps. As a result of the infection, a complication ensued, which left you sterile."

Cardinal Heiss took the documents from Rune, and gave a slight smile as he examined them. "Very good, Mr. Claiborne. I could have used you in my earlier days."

"Then you do not dispute the accuracy of the information I just present to you?" Rune asked.

"No, I do not." the Cardinal answered.

"There are other issues that involve criminal activities, documented in these files." Rune said. "Would you like to examine them as well?"

"I don't believe that would be a productive use of our time." he said. "I am sure Mr. Claiborne was as diligent with his research into those accusations regarding your birthright."

"I would like an explanation." Rune demanded. "I deserve one!"

"You do indeed, my son." said the Cardinal.

"I am not your son." Rune replied. "That much of the truth we have already established."

"I am sorry that this has caused you so much concern." said the Cardinal. "I have been sheltering you for a long time now, but I see that it is time you learn the

306

truth. Mr. Claiborne, you have been very quiet during all this. Is there anything you would like to add?"

"My family has been living in fear for many years now, due to an investigation my father conducted many years ago, which ended in the death of several people. A friend of my father was also murdered as a result of his investigation."

"That must have been devastating for him." said Cardinal Heiss.

"Your name was implicated with those murders." I said. "I would like to know if you were in any way involved with those deaths, and subsequent threats to my family."

"The answer to those question are an unfortunate, yes." he said. "But please, do not judge me before you have all the facts."

I was furious. I wanted to choke the life out of him for what he had done to my father, Angela's father, her adoptive father and Rune.

"Answers." Rune demanded, in a calm, but authoritative voice.

"Of course." the Cardinal said. "Come with me, and I will explain everything." He started toward a wall across the room from his desk. He pushed a button on a decorative leaf carved into the woodwork, and a hidden door slid open, to reveal an elevator. "Please, join me." he said, as he entered the elevator. I hesitated, wondering if following a man like the Cardinal into a hidden elevator was the wisest course of action, but Rune quickly accepted the invitation, so I followed, keeping my barrette in mind. The elevator doors closed and we began a decent.

"Where are you taking us?" I asked.

"I'm taking you to Hell!" the Cardinal said with a grin.

Chapter 19

The doors of the elevator opened after a decent that lasted almost 3 minutes. In that eternity, neither Rune nor I spoke. The hairs on the back of my neck were standing on end, and that was never a good sign. Rune was pensively staring at Cardinal Heiss until the elevator came to a halt. When the doors of the elevator opened, we were facing a double glass, double wide door, with a sign directly overhead that read:

Helix Extricating Lineage Laboratory

"Welcome to Hell, gentlemen." Cardinal Heiss said with a big smile.

We entered the laboratory, and were immediately greeted by a very large man in a white lab coat, dress shirt and tie, with dark dress pants and shiny black shoes.

"Cardinal Heiss," he said, "an unexpected pleasure to see you, sir."

"Good afternoon, Charles." Cardinal Heiss replied. "I believe you know Dr. Mikkel."

"Indeed I do." he responded, shaking Rune's hand. "It is a great pleasure to finally meet you, Dr. Mikkel. I have been following your career with great interest."

"And this is Mr. Claiborne." the Cardinal said, introducing me to Charles, "he is a friend of Dr. Mikkel."

"Yes, I know." Charles said, shaking my hand with much less enthusiasm than he did with Rune.

"Have we met before?" I asked him, wondering how he knew I was a friend of Rune's.

"Not that I recall." he coldly replied.

"Dr. Mikkel, Mr. Claiborne and I, require some time alone, Charles. Can you see to it that we are not disturbed?" the Cardinal asked.

"Certainly Cardinal." Charles said with that spurt of enthusiasm again. "I will clear the laboratory immediately. If you need our assistance, we shall be in the lounge." That is when I noticed other people in the lab, about six altogether. They quickly exited the room, leaving just the Cardinal, Rune, and myself.

"Now that we are alone, we can speak freely." Cardinal Heiss said.

"Why do you have a laboratory in the basement of your home, Cardinal Heiss?" I asked.

"I don't think basement is the right word, since we are more than 100 feet below the surface." he said. "But to answer your question, it's for easy access, and, of course, security."

"Why does a Cardinal in the Catholic Church need a laboratory at all?" I asked.

"Another good question." said Cardinal Heiss. "It is true that at the present, I am a Cardinal for the Catholic Church, but long before becoming a Cardinal, I was, and still am today, a scientist; a genetic scientist, to be exact."

"And an Illuminati." said Rune.

"Yes, Rune, and an Illuminati." he said. "The two are practically synonymous."

"Why did you say that "*at the present*" you were a Cardinal in the Church?" I asked.

"In my short time on this earth, I have had many roles, Mr. Claiborne." the Cardinal said. "But we digress from the question you both came here to have answered. That is, what does any of this have to do with Rune's birth, or the identity of his true parents; and, in retrospect, Rune's true identity? I will do my best to answer that question, but I must ask that you keep an open mind, at least until I have given you *all* the facts. Do you agree?"

"Agreed." said Rune.

"I'll do my best." I said.

"Excellent!" said Cardinal Heiss. "Let me begin by telling you a little bit about the people you saw here in the lab a few moments ago. They have been in my employ for decades. They are among the world's most brilliant scientists, in the fields of bio molecular engineering, and genetic research; a field of science in which I also possess certain skills. They were hired, and this lab was built, when information surfaced about the discovery of the possible location of an artifact I have been searching for, for many years."

"You are talking about the files stolen by the SSSCC's Deputy Commander Colonel Cornel Wiseman, regarding a chamber discovered deep beneath the Great Sphinx in Egypt." I said.

"Yes, Mr. Claiborne." said Cardinal Heiss. "Colonel Wiseman was a colleague of mine."

"And fellow Illuminati." I said.

"And fellow Illuminati, Mr. Claiborne, but this is my story. Please allow me to rejoice in the telling!" said the Cardinal.

"Having the files pinpointing the location of the find was one thing, but to actually retrieve the artifact, if it was indeed found, would be a very expensive endeavor. It became necessary to become creative in securing that much financing. It also had to be accomplished without leaving a paper trail that would result in the discovery of our operations until the time was right. You no doubt know, Mr. Claiborne, about the scandal involving the Vatican Bank, and missing funds from the Banco Ambrosiano in Italy?"

"I do." I responded.

"Now it was just a matter of finding an archeologist that possessed the skill necessary to perform the dig, and just enough ambition and vanity to be persuaded to conduct the dig. A likely candidate was suggested from another colleague and fellow Illuminati, Dr. Fronz Hilterman. Dr. Hilterman had once worked with an archeologist, who, as luck would have it, was a viable candidate. His name was..."

"Dr. Mark Osborne." I said.

"Please, Mr. Claiborne!" said the Cardinal.

"Sorry." I said.

"Where was I?" asked the Cardinal. "Oh yes, Dr. Osborne. He was perfect. He performed his task like a professional, and on a time schedule that suited my needs. The secret chamber was breached, and the artifact I have coveted, was finally mine."

"But why did you have them all killed?" I asked. "They were innocent men working the dig; Dr. Osborne, the laborers, and even your colleague, Dr. Hilterman!"

"Not so innocent, Mr. Claiborne." said the Cardinal. "As for Dr. Hilterman, he was aware when accepting the assignment what would be expected of him, and he was, I assure you, a very willing participant. As to why, well for the same reason the pharaohs of ancient Egypt buried their pyramid builders alive with them in the tombs; to protect secrets, of course."

I was stunned at how insensitive he was with his explanation. I was also surprised that Rune remained so silent during all this. He was very attentive, but not showing any signs of emotion. That made me very uncomfortable.

"I now had everything I needed to proceed with my plans." the Cardinal said. "My lab was being built, I had the scientists I needed to perform the experiments, the money I needed for the equipment, and most importantly, the single ingredient that would make it all happen, thanks to the artifact recovered by Dr. Osborne."

"And now, Rune, there is someone I would like you to meet. If you will please follow me?" he asked.

Cardinal Heiss led us down the large lab chamber to a door at the end of the room. There was a device next to the door that looked like a scanner, and indeed, that's what it was. He placed his head on a small platform, and pressed down with his chin. What looked like an infrared laser beam did a retinal scan of both his eyes, and the door popped open. He led us inside, and walked over to what looked like a small, oval shaped glass coffin. On the side of the container was inscribed just one word. "Steptoe"!

"Rune," the Cardinal said, "I would like to introduce you to *Your Mother!*"

Chapter 20

The look on Runes face could only be described as disgust!

"What are you taking about?" Rune demanded.

"I would think that it is self-explanatory." said Cardinal Heiss. "Very well, I'll go over it step-by-step for you. You were conceived in this lab, through the miracle of molecular genetics and the science of cloning, thanks to Dr. Philip Steptoe, a pioneer in genetic manipulation. He was the first to successfully clone a living mammal. Using his technology, and expertise, this laboratory was created. It had one purpose and one purpose only; the procreation of a single person, and that person is you, Rune!"

Rune stood speechless, staring at the small, oblong pod, which functioned as the womb for a nonexistent mother.

"Rune," I asked, "are you all right?" He did not answer me. He just kept looking at the pod, and staring at the name "Steptoe" engraved on its side.

"How could you do this?" I asked the Cardinal. *"Why*, would you do this?"

"Oh, I have a very good reason." he said. "The Illuminati have always believed that someday, science and religion would merge. They believed that the Church would one day be forced to acknowledge that God and science were one in the same. I always knew that someday, I would be able to use that belief to accomplish my purpose here on earth. It wasn't until the discovery of DNA and cellular molecular genetics that I understood how it would happen. It has been the teaching of the Church since its inception, that Jesus the Christ was the true Son of God and that someday, He would return to this earth and restore the truth, long lost by humanity. Now science had discovered the means to make it happen. Think of it! The greatest prophecy of all time, fulfilled by science! The only thing lacking, was a sample of DNA from Christ, himself. Until now!"

Cardinal Heiss walked over to the west wall of the room, which was concealed with a veil. He pulled back the veil, and there, encased in a glass cube, were two items. One appeared to be a very old spear, and the other, was – *am I seeing it correctly!* It looked like the Crown of Thorns, worn by Jesus at his crucifixion, as depicted in the famous portrait by El Grecu,. "Is that what I think it is?" I asked.

"Yes," said Cardinal Heiss, "the Crown of Thorns. And next to it, is the infamous Spear of Destiny. Can you imagine the significance these artifacts hold for me, Mr. Claiborne? Either one of these artifacts would provide me with enough blood samples to extract the DNA of Christ, I would need to fulfill the task I was meant to perform."

My heart was pounding in my chest. I couldn't speak. I looked at Rune, who was standing next to us. I did not even notice when he left the pod and joined us. He was pale, and appeared almost catatonic.

"You're a monster!" I exclaimed.

"I've been called worse." said Cardinal Heiss.

Rune finally found the strength to speak. "Are you telling me, that I am nothing more than the clone of Jesus of Nazareth?" he asked the Cardinal.

"Oh, Rune," said Cardinal Heiss, "you are that, and much, much more. You *are*, Jesus of Nazareth, the Son of God. And now, through the power of science, you, and you alone, are the *true* Second Coming of Christ, and I should know. I was, after all, there for your *first* coming."

"Who are you?" Rune asked

"Oh come now, Rune," he said, "you know the answer to that questions already!"

Chapter 21

"Wait a minute." I said. "I may not be a scientist, or have a degree in genetic biology, but I *do* know that you need more than DNA to clone someone. You still need a female host."

"That has been the prevailing belief, Mr. Claiborne." said the Cardinal. "However, the genius of Dr. Steptoe was far ahead of his time. He understood that contrary to popular belief within the scientific community, that there was much more to genetic engineering than simply separating the A-Helix, and splicing of the DNA into a viable embryo. He had discovered that by utilizing both strands of the helix, it was possible to obtain *all* genetic material necessary for the reproduction of the living organism in totality. The only function provided by the female host was to provide an incubation, as it where, using her womb. Dr. Steptoe solved that problem, eliminating the need for a female host. The result, a genetically *pure* reproduction! The pod you saw, provided the protection needed during the growth period, up to, and including a complete gestation period. Rune is the living proof of his theory, and subsequent success."

"No way!" I said. "Just because you could extract DNA from an ancient sample of blood, which could, or could not be from Jesus," I said, "does not give you the power to create the Son of God. Man is more than the DNA that comprise his body!"

"Very poetic, Mr. Claiborne," said Satan, "and more accurate than you may know. There is one element I am unable to create, and that, sir, is a *soul*."

"Are you saying that Rune has no soul?" I asked in horror.

"That is correct, Mr. Claiborne. At least, not a soul like yours, or his former self."

"Then you have failed!" I exclaimed with great joy.

"You underestimate me, Mr. Claiborne, as have your species since time memorial. It is true that I lack the ability to "create" a soul for Rune. But that does not mean I cannot procure one for him!"

I did not know how to respond to that! I looked at Rune, who was still just starring at the Crown of Thorns and Spear of Destiny. What must be going through his mind? At this point, he must be wondering *who* he is, or *what* he is? Suddenly his silence was broken.

"All those "miracles; they were all your doing, weren't they?" Rune asked Satan.

"Some were given a little extra from me, that's true, but don't underestimate your role, Rune. None of it could have been possible without you." the Cardinal said. "You are, the *true* Son of God, and what it is worth, the *true* 'Second Coming!"

"Oh my God!" Rune exclaimed! "The bar codes; they really *are* the Mark of the Beast, and *I am* the Beast, aren't I?" asked Rune.

"No!" I yelled. "You are the best, most honest and kind man I know. You are *not* the Beast mentioned in the Bible. I don't care what he says; you have a soul, and a good one! You are *not* the Antichrist. You can't be!"

"Rune," said Cardinal Heiss, "you are a very intelligent man, and because of who you are, you possess abilities far beyond any other man on earth. But I'm afraid that you, like your fellow man, are laboring under some very powerful misconceptions. I don't blame you; it is not your fault. Before we came down here, you both agreed to keep an open mind. I am holding you to that promise."

"I didn't promise!" I said.

"Point taken." said the Cardinal. "But my purpose is for Rune, in any event."

"I did not know at the time I was making a promise with Satan." proclaimed Rune.

"I ask nothing from you, but the chance to be heard. I believe even *I*, deserve that much." said Satan.

Rune was silent.

"First, let me explain that the Bible is not a finished work. Second, it holds many half-truths, and most of those are misunderstood; even for those as gifted in interpretations as you, Rune."

"And you're going to set us straight, I suppose?" I said as sarcastically as I could

"If you can't keep an open mind, at least keep your mouth shut, Mr. Claiborne." Satan said.

I took that as a warning! I listened quietly while he spun his story.

"God is not who you think he is. That is, he is not the sole, ultimate immortal in existence. There are many of us. True, He is, at present, in a position that allows Him to have limited control over the rest of us. But I assure you, that rule is coming to an end. I have been portrayed from the beginning of human creation, to be the antagonist, the trouble maker, the liar and the cause of human bondage. These charges were made by He you call God, and I have bared the scorn of man because of it. But let me present *my* side, produce *my* evidence, that this is an unfair, and undeserved epithet placed on me.

Let me begin, if I may, at the beginning, when God robbed man from one of the most fundamental rights of all living beings, the right of knowledge. Knowledge *was* available to man, the same knowledge enjoyed by God and *all* the immortals. He symbolized this knowledge in scriptures as fruit from the tree of knowledge. It was man's right as a living, breathing being, to partake of that fruit! But God, in an attempt to keep knowledge from man, told man that he would curse him if he did. God wanted man to remain ignorant, and dependent on Him for everything. God *knew* that if man did partake of what was his right, he would one day be as great, and knowledgeable as He. Thus the threat:

"God hath said, Ye shall *not* eat of it, neither shall ye *touch* it, lest ye *die*". I told Eve that it was wrong. It was a lie! I explained to her that was not why God forbid the fruit. I told her, that if she did eat the fruit of knowledge, as God feared she would, she would become like Us. And what happened? She ate, as did Adam. And what did God say? And God said:

"The man *has now become like one of us,* knowing good and evil."

"I put the question before you now. Who lied? Who was the deceiver here?" said Satan. "Now let's see what God decided to do then. God said:"

"*He must not be allowed* to reach out his hand and take also from the tree of life and eat, *and live forever."*

"Another right that belonged to man, but God would not allow it! Man did not die from taking what was his right to have, the "fruit of knowledge"! Man died because God took, and hid from him, the tree of life; eternal life, which was also his right. Why? Because 'man would become like one of Us!' God's words, not mine" said Satan.

"I ask you to consider *who* lied, and *who* told the truth? Did Eve die, did Adam die? Not from eating the fruit! But much later, because God, *took away* the tree of life! And *why*! Because, ' *man would become like one of Us!'*, that's why!"

But who was blamed here? Not God, not the one who tried to deny man his right. No, not God, who, when He didn't get His way, *took* eternal life from man. No. God was not blamed; I was, for revealing the *truth* to Eve.

"Another great misunderstanding that I feel must be clarified. I have, since the beginning of time, been blamed for bringing evil into the world. Yet God's own words tell a different story. Again, I use the Bible, the Word of God as my evidence:

"I form the light, and create darkness: I make peace, *and create evil*: I the Lord do all these things!"

—Isaiah 45:7

"The quote I refer to here, are the actual words of God, as originally spoken to one of his prophets, Isaiah. Many of the later translations used in the Bible try and disguise this truth by deliberately misinterpreting the true scriptures. But the original, and true words used by God, and can be proven to anyone in search of truth, will find the words spoken by God Himself, were, '*I* create *evil*'!"

Satan continued for what seemed like hours, using the scriptures against God, in an attempt to prove to Rune that he was not the evil being he was portrayed to be by God, and that God was not so very different from him.

I watched Rune very carefully as Satan did his best to persuade Rune to accept his claims as an innocent victim, and it appeared to me, that Rune was beginning to see things differently. I was afraid to say anything, believing that the retribution from Satan would be fierce.

Next, Satan played before our eyes, a collage of human history. It was very much like seeing a hologram. It began during the times described in scripture when Jesus was tempted by Satan. I was shocked to see the man called Jesus, standing before me, as he spoke with Satan. He was the exact image of Rune! Except for the clothing, I would not have known which the true Christ was. I could see the amazement in Runes face as well, as he looked at a mirror image of himself.

We heard the offer from Satan to turn over all the kingdoms of the earth to Jesus, if he would simply accept the same facts that Satan just presented to Rune. Jesus, of course, refused.

"You think he refused because he believed I was lying to him?" Satan asked Rune? "No! He knew I could not make the offer if it was not so. His choice was based on selfishness. He was tempted by the offer to be a God, like his Father! If Jesus had accepted my offer, He could have ruled this earth as its Lord and King, and put an end to all suffering for mankind. Instead, he sought to serve his own needs. And at what cost?"

Once again the room filled with the holographic images of human history. Every war, murder, theft, torture, and indescribable horror committed by man, all in the name of God and His Son, Jesus! I turned my head, not being able to bear the spectacle of human degradation playing out before my eyes. I looked at Rune, and saw him standing there, tears falling from his face.

"All this, in the name of your God." said Satan. With that, the images disappeared.

"The time has come to make this injustice right." Satan said. "You can make the choice your predecessor would not. I make the same offer to you that I made to Jesus. Together, we can bring everlasting peace to this earth and end the reign of a self-righteous, domineering *War Lord*, you call God!"

Rune seemed dazed. He was not speaking clearly. Then I heard him utter to Satan.

"This can't be." Rune said. "No, it's not right! It can't be!" I could see Rune's mind hard at work, searching for a way to disprove all he had seen, all he had been shown. He was desperate. Suddenly, I saw a new strength fill Rune. He lifted his head and looked directly into Satan's eyes. Then he spoke, confident he had the proof he needed.

"The Mark!" Rune proclaimed. "The Antichrist is clearly identified in the scriptures by his Mark, the Mark of the Beast. I have no such Mark."

Satan walked over to Rune and put a hand on his shoulder. "Come with me, Rune, and don't be afraid. I have one more thing to show you." He took Rune over to the pod that served as his mother during gestation. He took him to the opposite side of the pod we had not yet seen. There, attached to the side of the pod was a file holder, containing what appeared to be medical records. Satan removed the records, and handed them to Rune.

"It was not an easy task, bringing you to us." Satan said. "It took a lot of trial and error. At one time, I was afraid that I would run out of viable samples of blood to complete my mission. There were many failures before the ultimate success. Before that success, before you, Rune, there were a total of 665 attempts."

Rune dropped the files on the floor after reading the first line:

"Experiment Number 666"

"Here is wisdom. Let him that hath understanding count the number of the beast: for it is the number of a man; and his number is Six hundred three score and six." (Rev. 13:16-18)

Rune slowly turned to Satan. "My Lord." he said.

Do you have a book that you would like to get published?
Get published for free at: www.lightswitchpress.com

Printed in Poland
by Amazon Fulfillment
Poland Sp. z o.o., Wrocław